A Pumpkins' Halloween

Mark Kasniak

Please sign up for my mailing list to receive free giveaways, notification of pending promotions and information about my upcoming releases. You can sign up here.

http://eepurl.com/bKt0Wr

A PUMPKINS HALLOWEEN

It was just before dusk when the old woman lit the first of five candles being careful to place it firmly in the center of the carved out pumpkin turning it into a jack-o'-lantern. The late October night's air was crisp and slightly breezy causing the skin on her forearms to rise into gooseflesh and with it she wished she would've remembered to put on a sweater before heading outside to light the pumpkins.

From behind the old woman weak gales pushed dry brittle leaves across the front yard of her old comfortable home as by now almost all of the trees throughout the neighborhood had their branches barren of leaves. With their new found nakedness, they waved their liberated skeleton to and fro in ghoulish manners.

The candle she had lit flickered brightly at times, weakly at others, as it struggled to sustain itself. As the flame took deeper hold on the wick, the candle's paraffin wax began melting into hot drips that gave off the sweet smell of cinnamon. With the torch now securely sheltered inside the gourd, its heat quickly grew vertically only to begin burning the flesh at the very top of the pumpkin, adding an aroma of freshly baked pumpkin pie which then mixed with the cinnamon of the candle's scent.

The old woman had just lit a second candle when her husband peered out from the doorway, then ambling out onto the front porch saying, "Why do you even bother with that nonsense? Every year with this stuff... Do you enjoy punishing yourself or something? Come back inside. We'll turn out the lights, and forget all about this stupid holiday."

The old woman breathed a heavy sigh and went on about her business of lighting each of the jack-o'-lanterns, ignoring her husband, and blocking his criticisms out of her mind.

After the fifth and final gleaming face was aglow, the old woman went back into her home to gather her sweater just as the streetlamps came to life sending their yellow iridescent light out into the world.

The casting of the dim, mellow light created eerie shadows on the roadway that impressionable young minds would soon surely come to think would be hiding a troll, goblin, ghosts, vampires, all kinds of ghouls, and of course dreaded kidnappers. All of these monsters were possibly lurking on this night, the one night of the year when the impossible, the unthinkable, became possible. The day the dead were supposedly believed to be allowed to come back and walk among the living, Halloween night.

"Ayah," one of the jack-o'-lantern yawned as if awakening from a deep slumber. "Yuk, is that cinnamon I taste? Oh, I hate cinnamon, why do I always get stuck with cinnamon?" he complained.

"Is that you Murray?" asked another one of the pumpkins.

"Yes, Ally. It's me."

"Stuck with cinnamon again, are you?" she giggled. "Oh, how you always hated cinnamon."

"Third year in a row, I swear she does it on purpose just to irritate me," Murray whined while doing his best to ameliorate the bad taste stuck in his mouth by sucking in large gulps of the cold fall air. With the influx of oxygen, his candle's flame twitched and burned even brighter, hotter, causing his head to fill even more with the pungent odor of freshly ground cinnamon sticks.

"Well, I got sour apple this year," said Ally while a warm glow emerged from deep within her core and shimmered outward making her carved out eyes twinkle. "Oh, how I love the smell of it, I wish it could last for the entire year," she then added as the soft light helped to perfectly contour the corners of her smile which only made her look even more mirthful than she already was, and she was very mirthful.

"What are you guys talking about?" a voice called out. "You didn't start without me did you?"

"Henry, is that you?" asked Ally.

"Yes, it is I," replied Henry.

"Hello, Henry," Murray said with a touch of sourness in his voice.

"Oh my, Murray, I didn't recognize you, not with all those bumps and warts covering your face like that," Henry snickered back in a playfully sarcastic tone. "I guess she picked the perfect one out for you this year. It fits your personality like a glove, cranky and wretched."

"Yes, well… we can't all be a smiling little princess like Ally here, believing that the world is full of cookie making elves and unicorns with rainbows shooting out their bum."

"Henry, did you overhear that Murray got stuck with cinnamon yet again?" Ally said giggling at the notion for a second time.

"Why yes, I did," Henry quipped. "Third year in a row isn't it, Murray? That's wonderfully fantastic! You having always hated cinnamon and getting stuck with it yet again, couldn't have happened to a bigger jerk."

"You know, Henry," Murray responded with

derision in his voice. "You should consider yourself lucky I don't have arms, or I would berate you like I used to. Do you remember, Henry, how I would beat you senseless just for the fun of it?"

"Yes, well, all in the past now, isn't it?"

"Henry, what kind of candle did you get this year?" asked Ally.

"Oh, I do believe its banana, or some other type of tropical plantain."

"Oh, how wonderful," Ally said cheerfully. "I remember how we would always have a banana packed in our lunches every day. They were so good. Oh, how I do miss them. You know who used to love them? April. Oh, how she used to beg us all for ours. I swear, she would've sold her soul to you if you had a banana to give her."

"Yes, well, April was always a rather rambunctious child, always taking everything to the extremes," stated Henry. "Speaking of April, is she here yet?" he then asked as he was placed just slightly on enough of an angle to make it difficult for him to see April who was in line right next to him.

"Yes, Henry, I'm here," answered April.

"Oh, April," rejoiced Ally, her flame flickering and giving off a wavering light which made her look as if her eyes were darting back and forth.

"Have you been with us long? We were just talking about you."

"I've been here, but for only a few minutes," responded April. "I hadn't realized my candle was lit until just now, but I have been here long enough to hear that Murray got stuck with cinnamon again, couldn't have happened to a bigger prick."

"That's what I said," proclaimed Henry enthusiastically.

"All right, all right, already," Murray huffed. "If you two don't knock it off with calling me a male phallic, I'm going to blow out both of your candles and be done with the two of you for another year."

"Okay, okay, calm down Murray," April stated.

"April, was Tilly with you?" asked Ally.

"Yiim ear," responded Tilly in her small elfin like voice, her speech having been slurred on account of the old woman having carved her face upside down.

"Oh, Tilly… Are you all right?" asked Ally as she tried desperately to control her laughter. "You sound positively drunk. Are you going to be talking that way all night?"

"Aye ope n-not. B-But th-years n-not mutch Ay-an-doo."

"Well, you sound positively silly," April quipped will also cracking a giggle. "But then again, you were always the silly one, weren't you? I suppose that's why she carved you out that way."

"mmyeehbe," responded Tilly.

"What type of candle did you get this year, Tilly?" asked Ally.

"Ay tink wawamelun," Tilly stammered.

"All right, all right now!" shouted Murray. "Ally, that's enough with the candles. You're obsessed with the candles."

"Oh, shut it, Murray!" Ally snapped back. "You just got your panties in a bunch because you got cinnamon again."

"Ah-ha," giggled Tilly. "Ats tree ears inn ah r-oh."

"Ats tree ears inn ah roh," Murray repeated mocking Tilly. "At least I don't sound like I've got a mouthful of marbles. Are we going to have to listen to her talk like this all night? I won't be able to bear it."

"Ay'mm oohing ma bess," answered Tilly.

"WHAT?" Murray demanded.

"She says she's doing her best, Murray, now leave her alone," April said coming to Tilly's aid.

The old woman suddenly came back out on the porch with a large bowl filled with candy—miniature Snickers bars, M&M's, Butterfingers, Twizzlers, and Mounds could be seen all mixed throughout. She then set the bowl on the porch railing where the jack-o'-lanterns sat holding their silence until she went back inside the house.

"Mounds bar Yuk!" Murray grumbled. "They still make those?"

"I rather like them," said Ally.

"Ay ikem tuu," Tilly agreed.

"I thought I told you to be quiet, Tilly," chided Murray.

"Oh, knock it off, Murray," April chided, as she tried sticking up for Tilly again. "You don't need to be so mean to her. You were always so mean to her."

"Why don't we just start the stories," added Henry.

"How can we get on with the stories, you twit," berated Murray. "There not even any trick-or-treaters yet."

"You don't always have to be so mean, Murray," said Ally clearly also irritated by Murray's boorishness.

"You don't always—," Murray began.

"Shut up, shut up, they're coming back," April said, interrupting Murray after she saw that the old man and the old woman was exiting the house and coming out on the porch. As they neared, the old man could still clearly be heard continuing on with his complaints about the old woman's insistence on celebrating the holiday.

"Why do you even bother with all this?" the old man griped in a frustrated voice. "Everything you put up, you're going to have to take down and put away again. All that work for nothing. And, all these kids will be coming here onto our property. You know one of them will surely trip and fall over their own two feet, and then we'll be facing a lawsuit. You know I'm right. That's all *these* people do nowadays is sue each other over everything, even when it's their own brats fault for not being able to walk properly."

"Oh, will you knock it off already?" the old woman said shaking her head at the old man. "That's all you ever do anymore is piss and moan. It's only one day a year and I like to see the children all dressed up in their costumes. They're so cute, the little ones."

Ally laughed a little when she heard the old woman giving it to the old man, and then she uttered, "Go get'em, that old grump," in a whisper low enough so that the old couple wouldn't hear her.

"Shut up, you moron," mumbled Murray under his breath. "You're going to get us caught, and then will have to leave."

At the end of the yard, not far from the street, the old man struggled to get his old legs up a step stool he had haphazardly placed on an immense tree root that shot out from a mammoth maple. Once shakily standing atop the highest step while weakly holding onto one of the trees branch's with a frail hand, the old woman then handed him a cartoonish looking bat that hung from a string. The bat had bright green googly eyes and a playfully wide smile. When the old man turned on a switch hidden on its bottom the bat began shaking vigorously giving off a little dance as it dangled from its thread. As the bat cavorted, it emanated a spooky "wooooo," meant to scare little children into the spirit of the holiday.

"Oh, look," proclaimed the old woman. "I think I see a few of the children coming down the street already. It looks like they're already starting."

"I don't want them on my property," the old man groaned as he got down from the stool somewhat wobbly. "I just know one of them is going to hurt themselves on that crack in the driveway, and they'll walk right through the flower beds to get to the next house instead of walking around the yard using the sidewalk like they're supposed to do."

"Oh, all right then, you old fart!" the old woman snapped at the old man dismissively. "Go and get a couple of chairs from the garage and we'll sit at the end of the driveway and pass out the candy from there."

"*We'll* pass out the candy?" objected the old man. "Why do *I* have to stay out here, passing out candy? It's cold out."

The old woman just gave her husband a dour look. With it, the old man then acceded to her wishes letting out a labored shrug before heading off to the garage to retrieve the lawn chairs she had asked for along with a blanket large enough for the two of them.

It wasn't long until the first of the children made their way down the street to the old couple's house. The sounds of their young voices shouting trick-or-treat quickly beginning to fill the cool autumn air.

The old woman and the old man settled in snugly close to one another, sharing the blanket near the edge of the driveway, the old woman with the bowl of candy in her lap.

"It's getting pretty dark, and it seems that there is a fair amount of trick-or-treaters out now, so why don't we begin?" suggested Murray. "Whose turn is it to go first anyways?"

"Ay ink is myine," answered Tilly.

"No! No!" shouted Murray at the very thought of Tilly telling a story. "I won't be able to take listening to you butcher a story the way you sound—No Way."

"Ura yierk," countered Tilly.

"Yes, well... *too ba,* ''" rebuffed Murray.

"Why don't you go first this year, Henry?" asked April. "I've always liked your stories, they're so interesting."

"Alright," answered Henry. Then his candle suddenly began burning brightly as if he had willed it to do so, and it soon wafted the scent of banana into the air that lingered. "Who will pick for me?"

"I shall pick for you," Murray replied answering for everyone. "Now let's see...," he then said as he gazed out into the yards and street at the different groups of trick-or-treaters. "Army guy, no... Cowboy, no... Bloody doctor, no... Vampire, no..."

"Do the vampire!" April called out enthusiastically. "I would love to hear a story about a vampire."

"No! No...," said Murray. "It's my pick, so I get to choose."

"Well, pick one already," said Ally impatiently.

"Yeaah!" Tilly concurred.

"Okay, okay, already. Ahhh... here we are, a princess, perfect for you, Henry," Murray said snickering.

"Ha, you don't think I can do a story about a

princess, do ya?" Henry countered. "Well, prepare to look foolish, Murray, even more than you already do."

Henry wasted no time going into his story.

Her name is Erin, and her story doesn't begin tonight. Her story actually began a week ago while she was sitting on her bed. It was her birthday, and she had just turned seven. She was busy going through the contents of an old shoe box, and she was crying. In her hand she held a photograph of her and her mother, they were in their backyard next to a rose garden, and her mother had her arms around her, holding her tightly. Erin remembered every moment of that day. How the sunlight warmed her skin, the sweet smell of honeysuckle in the air, the rhythmical buzzing of a humming bird's wings that had flown into the yard only fleetingly right before her father had taken the picture. That day was two years ago now, and seventeen months before ovarian cancer had taken her mother.

Erin wiped her eyes with the palms of her hands and then blotted them dry on her bed sheets. She then reached into the box, pulling out a dried up withered rose, careful to hold it delicately so none of its pedals broke off the stem. The rose had come from the rose garden in the backyard, picked personally by Erin herself, to be placed on her mother's casket at the funeral. Erin situated the flower on the bed next to the picture and then continued to pull more items from the box. There was a locket Erin's mother had given her. At the time when Erin's mother had bequeathed it to her, she said that she was right around the same age Erin was then when her mother had given it to her. There was also a ticket stub from the time they went to the circus and the both of them had gotten their faces painted to make them look like a couple of clowns. And, at the bottom of the box was a ribbon Erin's mother used to wear in her hair. It still smelled somewhat like her.

"*Hey,* sweetheart," Erin's father said as he stood in the doorway, peering into the room. "What's the matter, why are you crying?" he asked her in a soft voice, but then noticed the box and Erin's picture of her with her mother that lay inside. He sat down next to her on the bed. "You really miss her, huh?"

"*Yeah,*" Erin said, wiping her runny nose with the back of her hand. "It's not fair."

"I know, I know," her father told her as he held her. "*Hey,* what do you say we go to the store and pick out your Halloween costume? You've always loved Halloween; it might make you feel better to get out of the house for a while."

"Yeah, I guess so," Erin agreed as she finished wiping the tears away from her face, her spirits sounding as if they were picking up already.

"Alright, sweetheart... but first I need you to do something for daddy."

Erin's father got up off the bed and began to unbuckle his belt.

"Daddy, No!" Erin began to sob again. "I don't like that, stop."

"Are you telling *us* that this sicko is diddling his daughter?" asked April.

"Would you let Henry tell his story and quit interrupting?" Murray chided her. "You always did that... *always* with the questions, *always* with adding your two cents."

"Well, *excuse me,*" April responded contentiously. "Please, go on Henry."

But before Henry could go on, from up the road came a group of teenagers barely dressed in costumes for the holiday. They were all wearing different types of sports jerseys while holding inexpensive plastic bags from a grocery store. They had approached the old man and the old woman who still sat nestled in their chairs at the end of the driveway. "Trick-or-treat!" they shouted at the old man and the old woman at a level that was clearly more than needed. The old woman suddenly startled, let out a small gasp while putting a hand on her chest, showing herself clearly shaken from the shouts of the boys.

"Aren't you lads a little *old* to be trick-or-treating?" the old man said becoming snarky.

"Ah, no!" replied one of the boys sarcastically.

The old woman then reached into her bowl of candy pulling out one of the treats before offering it to the nearest boy at the end of an outstretched arm. She then said with a smile, "Here you are young man," and waited for him to open his bag.

"Awe, not Mounds, I want one of the Snickers," cried the boy with a tone of entitlement that suggested he'd felt that the world needs to kiss his bottom.

"*You'll* get what you get, you little puissant," said the old man.

"Hey, what's your problem?" asked another one of the boys seethed nodding towards the old man, his voice high-pitched and breaking.

The old man could clearly see the teen's heavy acne showing through all the face paint he wore of his school's colors, and upon gazing at the youth's pimply face his own face became embittered.

"Go on, *get* the hell outta here, all of you," snapped the old man as he feigned getting up to challenge them.

"*Whatever,* dude," snapped the teenager who had his face painted, and then he and his friends lumbered on to the next house having made sure they trampled straight through the old couples flowerbed that separated theirs from their neighbor's property.

"What a bunch of jerks!" cried Ally.

"Yeah, well, not much we can do about it, can we?" added Murray dismissing the situation. "It's over now anyway. At least they didn't get egged."

"Please go on with your story now, Henry," April said, speaking up and having wanted to change the conversation away from the rude boys. "You were at the part where Erin's perverted father was... was... Well, not being a very good father."

"Yes, so after Erin's father had finished with her he told her, 'Now don't you go being a ninny and telling anybody about what we've just done. That's a special secret shared only between daddies and their daughters. Nobody can ever know about it, okay?'"

"Okay," said Erin abjectly.

"Remember, if you ever talk about the special game we play, Mr. Mckutchin will get you, and you don't want Mr. Mckutchin to *get* you, do you?"

"No, daddy, I don't want *mean* old Mr. Mckutchin to get me."

"*Well, he won't,* as long as you keep our secret. Now, why don't you get your coat and your hat on, and we'll go down to *Party Town* to pick out your costume."

"Okay, Daddy," said Erin.

Mr. Mckutchin was known by all the kids in the neighborhood as being the creepy man to which they were all afraid of for reasons unbeknownst to them. Nobody ever saw him coming or going from his great big house that was across the street and a just a touch down the road from Erin's home. But, sometimes people, scary and furtive people, his ilk, would occasionally visit Mr. Mckutchin at night. They would pull their vehicles into the long, poorly lit driveway that led up to the eerie dwelling. Then, the cars would disappear into the house's garage as if being swallowed up whole.

Erin never saw anybody living there, not even so much as a landscaper occasionally tending to the brush and bramble that choked the front yard. But she had noticed the *'No Trespassing!'* sign that had been nailed to an old oak tree at the edge of the property. It clearly let everyone know they weren't welcome on Mr. Mckutchin's land.

Every once in a while, late at night, when Erin would look out her bedroom's window to stare at the old, capacious house looming in the shadowy darkness, she couldn't help but think of the place as a fortress or maybe even a prison that held its victims consisting of kidnapped, scared-to-death and crying children locked away deep within the belly of the house's basement. The mere sight of the dwelling ominously perched across the street would frighten Erin so much that she would pull down the window shade, hoping to block the image of the house from her mind so she could go to sleep.

The other kids in the neighborhood would also tell her stories about Mr. Mckutchin. They would say that he was a cannibal. That at night he would set out to kidnap children from other nearby towns. (Such towns, of course, nobody had ever heard of.) Then, after snatching up the kids he would lock them away in his dungeon where he would force feed them, making them fat and supple. His end goal eventually being the slaughter them and then consume their flesh, like a real life witch from Hansel and Gretel.

Other kids would like to tell stories that he was a Nazi war criminal still hiding out from the prosecution of his horrible crimes, and that he had mutilated and altered his face to hide his identity.

They had told Erin that, even though it has been many decades since the end of the war, Mr. Mckutchin still can't let go his enjoyment of the evil things he did during combat. And, if you listen carefully at night, you can hear the cries of anguish and torment coming from the people he tortures in his house. His killing spree forever living on in the form of his psychotic delusions and sick fantasies that he takes out on unsuspecting victims that he had convinced to show up at his house.

*****

When Erin and her father arrived at Party Town, Erin was feeling well again and in better spirits, and the sight of so many costumes to choose from had her feeling dizzy with excitement.

"I'm gonna be a ballerina. No, I'm gonna be a fairy. No, I'm gon—"

"Why don'tcha be something scary?" asked her father. "You're always supposed to dress as something scary on Halloween."

"No! I don't want to be something scary. I wanna... I wanna... I wanna be a princess."

"Okay, honey. Let's see what they have in princess costumes for my little princess."

Erin settled on a bluish purple gown with matching gloves and a tiara. She thought she looked just like Cinderella if only Cinderella had dark brown hair instead of blonde.

"I love it, I love it," she cheered aloud. "Can I get it, daddy? Please!"

"Of course you can sweetheart," her father told her.

Three days had passed since picking up the costume and Erin was counting the days down to Halloween on her calendar. "Just two more to go," she told herself as she put an "X" through the 29th with a big red magic marker.

As Erin sat in her room, she had heard her father come home from work that day in a huff and then go right to the refrigerator to grab a beer.

Erin knew not to bother her daddy whenever he came home from work and, at once, started drinking. She knew what his drinking would ultimately lead to, and, right on cue, a short while later Erin's father came looking for her up in her room.

"Honey, Erin, are you in here, honey?" he asked, leaning his head through the door.

Erin didn't say anything at first as she hid under her bed hoping he would just go away.

"Erin," he called out. "Where are you, sweetheart."

Knowing that he would eventually find her and not wanting to possibility make him mad because he had to go looking for her, Erin decided that it would be best if she just came out from underneath the bed and see what it was her daddy wanted.

"I'm here, daddy, I'm under here," she called out.

Grabbing the edge of the coverlet and flipping it up atop the bed, Erin's father looked underneath the mattress and box spring to see his little girl entwined between some old shoe boxes and a couple of stuffed animals.

"What are you doin' down there, honey?" he asked her in a calm fatherly tone. "Come on out and see me. I've missed you. Daddy's had a long, tough day at work, and I could use a hug and a kiss from my little angel."

Erin came crawling out from underneath the bed, even though she didn't want to, and her father then sat down atop of it, picking her up and placing her on his knee.

"You weren't hiding from me, were you?" he asked with a sad look on his face.

"No, daddy," Erin said.

She lied.

"Tell me about your day at school, sweetheart. Did everything go okay today?"

"Yeah, I guess so," Erin said with a sigh.

"That doesn't sound like everything's alright. Tell daddy what happened."

Erin paused for a moment not sure if she wanted to tell her father about the boy at school who had put gum in her hair today, and how the teacher, Mrs. Fallon had to cut it out with a pair of scissors. She just wanted to tell her father that she wasn't feeling right and that she wanted to go to bed early tonight. In the end, though, she did end up telling her father about the boy and the gum.

As she told her father all about the evil thing that Adam Schultz had done to her today in class, all because she wouldn't agree with him that Regular Show was better than Sponge Bob, Erin's father began sliding his hand up between her legs.

"Daddy, stop," she said, breaking away from her story. "I told you I don't like that!" she whined.

"It's okay, Erin," her daddy told her as he firmly but gently forced her legs back open. "Just keep telling daddy your story."

"No, I don't want to," she began to cry. "I don't feel well. I want to go to bed."

"Daddy wants to play our special little game for a while, and then you can go to bed, okay, sweetheart?"

Erin was visibly upset, but she knew there was nothing she could do about it. When daddy was upset, and been drinking, he was going to get his way. So, she just tucked herself away into a place deep inside of her where nobody could find her, where nobody could touch her, where nobody could hurt her.

Erin's father finished the game and then went to leave her bedroom so he could get a fresh beer, but on his way out he looked back at Erin saying, "Good-night, sweetheart, sweet dreams," to her before turning out the lights and heading downstairs. Erin then cried herself to sleep under the warm glow of her Winnie the Pooh night-light.

The next day on her way home from school, Erin had asked the bus driver, Mrs. Boyle, if she would drop her off at the end of her street where her friend Madison got off the bus because her father would be working late and she was to spend the evening at Madison's house until he came home. It was a lie, but Erin didn't think it was all that big of one.

The real reason Erin didn't want to go home was because she knew her daddy would be there and she didn't want to see him. She knew she couldn't hideout forever, but a little time at the park that was down the street she knew wouldn't have her father worrying himself to death.

Spinning in circles on the merry-go-round, a few trips up and down the slide, and then a little quality time on the swings, had done wonders for Erin's spirits.

As she swung on the swing ever higher and higher she dreamed that the swing would eventually reach the moon. A rubber mat seat and a couple of semi rusted up chains was all Erin needed to escape this world and to be able to get to far off places where she could hide. Places with no monsters, not bad guys, no daddies that liked to drink and play games with their little girls that required them to not wear any clothes.

Erin began pushing herself harder and harder on the swing with all her might, reaching ever higher into the atmosphere. With each upward stint, she had felt like she was about to lift off breaking the

Earth's gravitational pull on her. But, unfortunately though, each and every swing would ultimately conclude with her coming crashing back down again.

After all of Erin's energy had been spent trying to get her rocket ship to fly, she sat forlornly on the swing, and unhappily thought about how late it was becoming. She was sure that her daddy was looking for her by now, and most likely angry. She began to cry at the thought of her father being cross with her. How he would punish her for not coming straight home after getting off the bus, for making him worry.

She soon began to sob uncontrollably, and as she gasped for air, tears started streaming down her cheeks. She felt trapped, abject, utterly alone.

"Erin," a voice said. "Why are you crying, did you hurt yourself?"

Erin looked up, and a man stood before her with his dog that was on a thick leash. He was tall, like a giant, but had a kind face. Still, his freakishly abnormal size had taken her aback, frightened her till she almost screamed.

"I don't know you," Erin said as she wiped away her tears with the palms of her hands. "I'm not supposed to talk to strangers."

"Well, I know you," the man said. "And that's very good advice. You shouldn't talk to strangers; you never know what sort of bad people are out there." The man then offered her his handkerchief. "Did your father teach you that?"

"I have to go home now," Erin said nervously and got up off the swing. The man's dog then began sniffing her coat and then her hands.

"Very well then," said the man. "Perhaps maybe I should walk you home, you seem a bit upset.

"I already told you, I'm not allowed to talk to strangers." Erin whined, becoming even more agitated by the man's sudden presence.

"I all ready told you, Erin, I'm not a stranger," said the man giving her a subtle smile. "I live on your street, we're neighbors."

Erin looked up at the man quizzically. She knew he wasn't one of her neighbors like he said he was. She had never seen this man before, she would have definitely remembered him if she had. But, then it hit her, Mr. Mckutchin.

Erin suddenly tensed up, she wanted to scream, but her voice abandoned her. She thought about running, but she knew she couldn't outrun the giant, and definitely not his dog. *This is it*, she thought to herself. What every kid in the neighborhood had lain awake at night afraid of. He's gonna lock me up in his basement and feed me bugs and rats until I'm fat enough for him to cook me up for dinner, and then he'll feed what's left of me to his dog.

Erin's eyes quickly became once again

embedded with the moisture of soon to be shed tears as she looked up at him in a frozen suspension of fear.

The man just simply reached out one of his lengthy arms, offering her his hand.

"Come along with me then Erin if you're not to hurt to walk. It gets dark early this time of year, and you should probably be getting home."

Erin took Mr. Mckutchin's hand and found that it was warm and gentle, just like she remembered her mother's used to be. They began walking together out of the park, his Great Dane, Morty, excitedly cavorting up beside her. The slobbering pooch was also an enormously huge thing, Erin thought. He reminded her of a horse, or possibly a donkey with his upturned ears. She watched as he ran around playfully, and had even thought fleetingly that he was as big and dark enough to be easily confused with a bear. She had also noticed that he had set of teeth on him that could strike fear into the hearts of the wickedest of bad guys. Erin wasn't afraid of him, though, not with the way he excitedly tried to play with her. She actually found herself comforted by his presence as they walked.

As they moved along together, the man who Erin was now assured of as being Mr. Mckutchin asked her again, "Did you hurt yourself back there on those swings?" to which Erin replied, "No."

A moment later she asked the tall, large man, "Are you Mr. Mckutchin?" in her small elfin-like voice, to which he replied, "People have called me that, yes."

"Did you have a bad day at school today, and maybe that's why you were crying?" asked Mr. Mckutchin looking down upon her with thoughtful eyes.

"No," Erin said somberly.

"Are you going to lock me up in your basement until I'm big and fat, and then eat me, and then feed my bones to your dog?" asked Erin in a tone which almost made her sound like she had already accepted her fate.

"Heavens, No," Mr. Mckutchin laughed out boisterously. "Is that what all the kids are saying about me? Well, I guess it's better than being a Nazi on the run who likes to torture people in his basement. I never quite found out who started that one."

Erin cracked a smile at Mr. Mckutchin when he laughed, and it was at that moment she knew he wasn't going to hurt her. She knew the stories that her father and the other neighborhood children had told her about Mr. Mckutchin were never true.

"Then, why don't you ever come outside your house?" she asked him quizzically.

"I'm outside right now, aren't I?" he answered.

Erin thought about his response and soon

recognized the erroneousness of her question. She then squeezed his hand a little tighter.

"Then why do you have that no trespassing sign on your lawn and all those bushes keeping people from seeing into your yard?" she asked.

"Ah ah-ah," Mr. Mckutchin then said. "It's my turn to ask you a question. Were you crying because you miss your mom? I know how hard it sometimes is to lose someone you love."

"No," Erin said lowly. "I miss my mom a whole lot, but I wasn't crying because of her."

"Well, I guess you've answered my question, so I'm obliged to answer yours now," Mr. Mckutchin stated. "I have that sign and those tall bushes because you're right, I don't want people coming into my yard, or any children creeping around my house for that matter, *especially children*."

Erin looked up at Mr. Mckutchin, not sure if she should pull her hand away from his after he revealed his distaste for children.

"You see, it's not that I don't like people or children," Me. Mckutchin then went on. It's just... It's just that my friends and I tend to partake in what I would call, *very special games*, games for grownups that is, and a very special few of them at that. It's not something I would like for people to see, especially children. And, at times, we can get very loud and rambunctious when we play our special games, so we try to keep our games hidden, if you can understand that, Erin. Do you have any special games that you like to keep hidden, Erin?"

Erin now pulled her hand away from him, not knowing what to say.

"Were you crying because of your dad, Erin? Were you crying because of special games he likes to play with you?"

*****

The next day was Halloween and Erin had found herself excited for its arrival all day long while she was in school. She had gotten a rare lucky break for once in the form of her father having come home late from work yesterday, so he hadn't found out that she'd gone to the park after getting off the school bus instead of coming straight into the house. That meant she didn't have to accept missing out on trick-or-treating as a punishment for her transgressions.

When Erin had gotten home from school, she at once ran into her house and then to her bedroom to put on her princess costume. Her father had told her that it was too early for her to be wearing her Halloween costume, that, trick-or-treating wasn't for another four hours, but she didn't care. Erin couldn't think of anything accept that today she was a princess and nothing was going to take that away from her. She even ate dinner in her costume, much to her father's dismay that she would end up spilling some of her sloppy Joe on it.

Soon after dinner the day crept into the night and the streetlights came on illuminating the roadway in their basking glow. Other kids on the block could already be seen making their way up to Erin's house, and she could hear their faint cries of, "TRICK-OR-TREAT!" coming from up and down the street.

Excitedly, Erin called out to her father telling him to, "hurry up" in fear that they would miss the holiday. It was as if she was foolishly worried about becoming little Sally Brown, who had missed Halloween after having been duped into hanging out all night in a pumpkin patch by the love of her life Linus van Pelt.

"I'm coming! I'm coming!" her father shouted down to her from the top of the staircase. "We've got plenty of time, no need to rush."

"But all the other kids are already out trick-n'-treatin' and if we don't hurry we'll miss it!" Erin whined back to her father.

"Alright, just give me a minute, for Pete's sake," he griped right back to her. "I still have to set out the bowl of candy because no-one will be here to pass it out while we're gone. And, lord-knows I don't need to come home to the house being egged."

Erin's father then quickly set out a bowl of

Snickers and Milky Way bars on an outdoor chair that he put in place close to the front door. He had left a note next to it instructing the trick-or-treaters to be on their honor and to take just one. But, he was confident that as soon as he and Erin turned the corner of the block the very first group of kids would have-at-it and that would be that.

Erin started her trick-or-treating with her next-door neighbor, Mrs. Annsteader, and then worked her way up the street. When she and her father had made their way back down the other side, Erin stopped before Mr. Mckutchin's house and stared into its dark, creepy yard.

"Pretty scary, isn't it?" her father said to her. "I wonder what creepy old Mr. Mckutchin is doin' in there tonight. Or, what creepy, old Mr. Mckutchin is doin' to one of his victims in there tonight," he then said in his best spooky voice before finishing off his sentence with, "Oooooo!" trying to sound like he was a scary ghost.

Erin didn't respond to her father's antics. She just looked at the house for a moment longer before turning her attention back to trick-or-treating.

Two blocks over Erin's bag was beginning to fill up and her father suggested that maybe they should start heading back for home. He told her that the Garfield and Peanuts Halloween specials would be on soon, and that it would be a shame if they had missed it. Erin agreed, and acceded to her father's wishes, her feet were starting to hurt from walking anyway.

On their way back, Erin and her dad had stopped at a house where its owners, an old couple, sat nestled comfortably together under a blanket near the end of their driveway as they passed out candy. Erin had taken notice of the five jack-o'-lanterns that sat in a row along the railing of the house's front porch, their candles giving off a supernatural flickering glow which illuminated their silly faces for the passers-by to see.

"Hey, look at that jack-o'-lantern up on the porch, Erin," her father said. "Check out the ugly one with all the warts and the stupid, grumpy look on its face, the one that reeks like cinnamon."

"Oh, hey, that's us!" shouted April excitedly. "Henry worked us into his story."

"Erin's father didn't say that when he and his daughter walked by!" grumbled Murray after having been affronted by his comments. "Quit being a jackass, Henry, and get on with your story or I'll make someone else go."

"Okay! Okay, so Erin had agreed with her father in that the particular grumpy looking jack-o'-lantern was truly the ugliest, most hideous Jack-o'-lantern she'd ever seen, and it positively reeked of cinnamon."

Erin had finished the block and then she and her father turned up the neighboring street heading for home. By the time they made it back, Erin couldn't have been more excited because it was her first chance to wide-eyed overlook and dig through her haul of candy, and saw it was a king's ransom at that. But before she knew it, she had only enough time to kick off her sneakers and grab two or three pieces of candy before Chuck, Peppermint Paddy, Linus, and Snoopy went on their Halloween adventure. An adventure Erin already knew would, ultimately, and predicatively leave Charlie Brown with a pile of rocks in his treat bag.

While Erin watched television up in her room, her father was downstairs also digging into *his* treats, a bottle of Johnny Walker Red and a fine cigar. Then, after about an hour of time had passed along with a four finger drop of the bottle's volume, he decided to go upstairs and check in on his daughter. There was still time before Erin would be fast asleep, he had thought to himself, and a round or two of their favorite game might just help him relax a little more than what the scotch had already done for him.

Erin's father had reached the top of the stairs, and as he approached her bedroom, he could see that the lights were still on inside the room. He then listened intently for a moment as he stood on the other side of the door and thought he could hear the sounds of people talking within, which he assumed must be the television.

After he had reached for the handle of Erin's bedroom door, he hesitated before going inside. For he suddenly recognized that the sounds he heard coming from within weren't emanating from the comedic banter of Garfield and Odie. No, it was the soft, sweet voice of Erin talking to someone as if there was another person in the room with her. Erin's father then slowly pushed his head through the door just enough to see inside and he instantly noticed that the television was left turned off, its screen blank.

"What are you doing, sweetheart?" he asked.

"I'm just playing with my friend," replied Erin.

Looking around the room and not seeing anyone with her, Erin's father assumed that her friend must be imaginary, so he decided to play along with the game.

"I don't see anybody, is your friend invisible or just hiding?" he asked stepping into the room.

"He's hiding," she giggled. "He likes to play games."

"He does, huh," her father replied, his arms akimbo, pretending to be upset with her. "I sure hope you don't have any boys up in your room, you're too young for that, missy," he then said, shaking a finger at her.

"No, daddy, we're just playing hide-and-go-seek," Erin responded with a beaming smile. He said he wanted you to play too.

"He did, did he?" Erin's father said as he got down on his knees to look underneath her bed. "Well, let's just see if I can find him." But underneath the bed laid nothing but the same collection of small boxes and stuffed animals he had seen a few days earlier when Erin was hiding.

"Nobody under there," he said.

"He's not under there," Erin said beginning to giggle again as she bounced up and down on the bed in excitement. "He's behind you, silly."

Erin's father turned around with an, "Ah-ha!" having expected to see absolutely nothing behind him, but still planning on pretending that her imaginary friend was standing there before him.

When Erin's father did spin around to look, though, to his surprise Erin's friend truly was standing there. And if he was imaginary, Erin's father was going to register a complaint with the Better Business Bureau about Don's discount liquors because that bottle of Johnny Walker they had sold him was clearly laced with something that had him hallucinating.

Before Erin's father stood a wall of a man, he was at least six and a half feet tall on the smallest of a guess, and no less than three hundred pounds. He had the physique of a brick-shit house and appeared tougher than steel. He wore black, leather boots that went up to his knees and a matching black leather jock that firmly hugged his enormous legs. A shiny chrome zipper could be seen stitched vertically in the front that would unlock access to what was clearly a small child's arm that he had packed away in between his tree trunk sized thighs. The jock strap, then worked its way up across his chest where it split into a 'Y' stretching over his collarbones. The leather outfit over his shoulders grew into thick, menacing pads with shiny metallic spikes piercing out from them. Left exposed from the outfit, were the man's saucer-like nipples that pierced outwardly and had painful looking chrome loops dangling through them. Finally, fastened on the man's head he wore a black leather mask fashioned with yet another chrome zipper that opened to the mouth port. The apparatus fit snugly over his skull much like that of a wrestler whom wanted to keep his identity a secret from the audience.

Erin's father's voice instantly failed him when he saw the giant standing in her closet.

He then managed to stammer out, "W-W-Who, w-whhoo aare youu?" as he began to shake, and feeling a sudden urge to pee himself.

Erin giggled again, and then said, "That's my friend, daddy. He wants to play with you. He calls himself *THE MACHINE*."

"What do you want?" Erin's father screamed at

the man, his voice suddenly coming back to him. "Stay away from me! Stay away from my daughter! I'm going to call the cops!"

The Machine just stood there and then dropped his black leather bag he had been carrying in his right hand. Out fell an array of extremely large dildos, whips, clamps, a chain of enormously large and studded anal beads, and some contraption that had the words THE DEVIL'S DARENGER written on the side of it.

Erin hopped down off her bed, taking her bag of candy along with her. She then walked past her father headed for the door. When she got to it, she turned around to look back over her shoulder at her father and said, "I'm gonna go downstairs to finish watching cartoons. You guys can finish playing your game up here." She then left, closing the bedroom door behind her.

Erin could hear her father yell for her from the other side of the door. "Erin! Wait… Don't leave! Be a good girl and tell your friend that I need to go with you!" But Erin wasn't listening. She was already halfway down the stairs humming a song to herself.

Erin fell asleep that night on the couch as she watched television in the living room, surrounded by piles of candy and empty wrappers. She had paid no mind to her father's screams and cries of agony and torment that were going on upstairs as she drifted off.

After that Halloween Erin's father never touched her again.

"Yeaaa!" cried April. "That was a good one, well-done, Henry."

"Yasz, En-ree, ay irrei iked tat un," said Tilly.

"Ugh, *please,* Tilly, will you shut-up!" griped Murray. "Your babble is like murder on my eardrums."

"Leave her alone, you old grouch!" April chided him. "How would you like being upside down all night?"

"Alright, alright," Murray said trying to lighten everyone's annoyance with him. "Yes, well-done, Henry, I really didn't think you could pull that one off, but you did a good job."

"Look at them!" exclaimed the old man to his wife. "Look at these boys wearing these namby-pamby costumes. What is this…? This Mind Craft stuff… Looks more like Mind-crap! Ha. Japanese garbage is what it is. Whatever happened to kids wearing good-old fashioned American boy's costumes, like Army guys, Count Dracula, and becoming a ghost by wearing an old sheet over their heads? Now it's all this wimpy love-e-dovie girly garbage."

"Oh, hush-up, you old grump," said the old woman.

"Ah, *hell,*" griped the old man getting up from

his seat. "I need a beer, and gotta take a piss. I'll be right back." He then ambled along up the driveway towards the house, leaving the old woman to pass out candy alone.

"Okay, Henry, so, it's your turn to pick, make it a good one," said Murray.

"Alright, let's see," said Henry as he looked over the neighborhood. "April, I think it will be your turn, and I choose for you, that young gentlemen over there across the street, the one wearing the surgeon's outfit all covered in blood. What's his story?"

"Well, alright," April began. "Let's see... His name is Timothy Barren and his story goes like this."

Timothy Barren was a kid with a lot of serious issues that had gone unchecked for far too long. The boy had a sick fascination with torturing animals for fun. He would secretly like to set out traps in his backyard and around the wooded lot to the rear of his home so he could catch his little unsuspecting victims as they went about their travels foraging for food.

Timothy commonly would use peanut butter as bait inside the metal cage traps he would set near the tall oak trees at the very edge of his yard. Then, when he would catch a hungry squirrel, he would get that feeling he craved so much, that feeling of absolute power running through his veins, adrenaline. Being able to play God for Timothy was better than Christmas morning, better than pizza, better than video games.

"Ah-ha, Got you!" Timothy cried out to the little-gray squirrel that found itself trapped and was scrambling around in circles, panicking inside of the metal cage. "You're Freaking Dead. **DEAD!**" he stated as he laughed in his sociopathic, sadistic way.

He then sat for a while poking at the poor helpless creature with a stick as he thought about just how he was going to carry out the animal's execution.

"I GOT IT!" he gleefully said to himself before running over to the shed located at the rear of his home's property.

A moment later he came back with a can of gasoline and a box of matches.

"I sentence you to death by fire," he said to the little-gray squirrel as he removed the cap from the can. He then splashed the gasoline onto the cage and the squirrel immediately started screaming with a high-pitched cry that gave away its fear. Mirthfully, Timothy then splashed even more on the little critter.

Timothy then put down the can and placed its cap on tight before standing over the cage with a wild look in his eyes. He then lit a match, striking it firmly off the side of the box. As the flame came to life he watched excitedly as the match's eruption flared up from his fingertips.

The squirrel continued to screech in terror and writhed in agony from the gas having gotten into its eyes. Timothy then dropped the lit match into the cage, and the fuel ignited with a pop, followed by a rush of heat, and then a burst of yellow and orange light.

As the squirrel burned alive the poor critter slammed itself into the walls of the cage, desperately trying to put itself out.

Timothy smiled.

The squirrel cried and heaved as its fur burned away and its flesh blistered and cooked. A stench billowed up from the cage that smelled of singed hair, and garbage that had been sitting out on a hot summer's day.

"Trial by fire," Timothy uttered in a whisper to himself.

The squirrel hitched one last time, then stopped moving all together, its body continuing to burn like a lamp.

After it was all over, Timothy buried the squirrel's chard-black corpse in a hole he dug near a few of the tall oak trees that were sporadically scattered in the empty lot next to his backyard. After he'd finished his dirty deed, he went into his house looking for dinner, having never thought of the little squirrel again.

"What are you going to be for Halloween

tomorrow, sport?" Timothy's father asked him as he sat on the other side of the kitchen table.

"I'm gonna be a crazy surgeon that butchers people!" Timothy said eagerly. "Mom said that she was going to get me a pair of scrubs from her work, and I'm going to cover it in blood and guts, and I'll have a bone saw and a stethoscope."

"Wow! Sounds pretty scary," his father replied in feign surprise.

That night Timothy dreamt about catching another squirrel in his backyard he could kill. He dreamed about having used his bone saw to have removed each of the squirrel's limbs from its abdomen as it tried to struggle to get out of the snares he would use to hold it in place.

The next day Timothy's mother came through with her promise of getting him a pair of hospital scrubs for his costume. When Timothy came home from school, he saw them lying on his bed and he went straight to work on putting together his costume. By the time the evening came, he was ready to burst with anticipation.

Timothy had managed to convince his parents through endless complaining that he was too big now to go trick-or-treating with either of them. But, the real reason Timothy was eager to go out alone was because he had already tucked away a half-dozen eggs, three rolls of toilet paper, and a bar of soap for greasing windows ready to go in his bag.

Reluctantly, Timothy's parents had eventually caved and agreed that he could go out without either of them as long as he went along with his friend Michael and Michael's older brother John.

Promptly, just after dusk, Timothy began making his way down the street, hitting up all the houses on the east side of the avenue as he made his way to Michael and John's house.

He quickly ate a chocolate bar and then gum drops as he walked from house to house, littering the wrappers on some poor schlep's lawn. As he downed the candy he thought joyfully about how much better it tasted than the casserole his mother had prepared for dinner that evening.

After Timothy had made his way up the street another two blocks, he stopped and stared at the open field that divided his neighborhood with Michael and John's.

He pondered if he should just cut through the field which would lead him to the dead-end at the far point of Michael and John's street. Timothy had figured that he could save at least fifteen minutes of walking by cutting through the field, but then had decided against the shortcut because it was just too dark to see where he was going. He didn't want to chance accidentally walking into the tarn, which sat somewhere almost directly in the center of the field.

Timothy continued walking down the street for another couple of minutes, eventually coming to the corner where a forlornly looking stop sign loomed under a streetlamp.

Suddenly! From the other side of the street, Timothy noticed Raymond Parker and Alan Harrison, two of the neighborhood's local bullies. They had a kid wearing a vampire costume cornered and were demanding that he hand over his trick-or-treat bag.

The vampire kid was not much bigger than what Timothy was, so it wasn't a big leap for Timothy to assume that if he kept heading towards them, he'd be their next victim.

Timothy quickly ducked behind a tree. He then watched and listened as the other boy began to cry and plead with the bullies not to give them his bag, but to no avail.

As Timothy watched what was happening, he fantasized about lighting Raymond Parker and Alan Harrison on fire like he had the squirrel the day before, but he knew for now they would have to wait. Someday, he thought to himself. Someday you two jerks will get yours. I'll kill you both.

The bullies had successfully negotiated, with the aid of a well placed punch to the gut, the rights to the vampire boy's trick-or-treat bag.

From behind the tree, Timothy watched as the boy slumped away, holding his belly in a hug and crying. It was just then that he remembered his eggs. Reaching down into his bag he grabbed two of them. He then glanced back over at Raymond and Alan, who still stood across the street under the yellow light of the streetlamp, digging into the vampire boy's bag for the good pieces of candy. Timothy decided to go for it and he dropped his bag to the ground before throwing the eggs at the bullies.

The first egg shattered in the street about five feet before Raymond and Alan, but it caught their attention. The second struck Alan in the shoulder, covering part of his neck and the side of his face in runny yolk.

"Ah! What the fuck!" Alan cried out. "Who the fuck did that?"

Timothy grabbed his bag of Halloween candy and started hauling ass back down the street.

"There!" shouted Raymond. "It was that little shit right there."

The bullies immediately gave chase to Timothy, and as Timothy ran away, he would periodically looked back to see how far behind they were. To Timothy's disappointment they were quickly gaining on him, and he was quickly becoming exhausted.

"We're gonna kill you, you little shit!" Timothy heard Alan scream at him.

A stitch suddenly began developing in Timothy's

side, the pain grew rapidly until it was excruciating, and he became forced to stop running. He looked back at the bullies and could see that they were only about fifty yards away. Oh, crap, I'm dead, he thought to himself, but then he looked to his right and noticed that he was back in front of the wooded field that divided his neighborhood with Michael and John's. He then noticed the bullies closing in on him, so being out of options, he plunged into the darkness of the field.

Timothy could hear Raymond and Alan still screaming obscenities at him as he ran through the over-grown weeds and nettles. He could barely see more than a few feet in front of him as he weaved around trees. The pond, he thought. I need to watch out for the pond.

"I'm gonna find you, and when I do, I'm gonna rip your arms off!" Timothy heard Alan yelling in the darkness, and he knew that they had entered the darken field after him.

Timothy once again looked back to see if he could see the bullies, but he couldn't. Then, when he turned his head to look forward again, his foot suddenly struck something in the shadows, a tree's root possibly or maybe a rock. He fell forward losing his balance and his bag of candy. He hit the ground hard and felt a splash of water and muck fly all over his face and Halloween costume.

"Awe," he whined to himself. *I must have fallen*

into the edge of the pond, he thought no longer being able to even see his hand in front of his face.

Timothy picked himself up and began wiping the mud from his nose's brim and eyes. He then intently listened for Raymond and Alan, but heard nothing. *They must have gone back to the street*, he thought to himself. He then knelt and searched the ground for his bag of candy. After having found it waterlogged with pond scum he griped, "Awwwe!"

Timothy decided to keep moving forward through the woods, he had figured that he was by now at least halfway through it already, and besides, if he went back the way he came Raymond and Alan might be waiting for him out on the street.

Soon, Timothy could see a light emerging through the bushes directly ahead of him. He thought it must've been coming from one of the homes in Michael and John's neighborhood, so he pushed on through the thicket, closing his eyes as he went so as he wouldn't get poked. When he came to the other side of the bushes, surprisingly, he found himself in a clearing but still in the forest.

The light he had seen came from a fire that burnt in the center of the clearing, and through its warm glow he saw a deer standing on the other side. Timothy stood completely still, staring at the buck and it did the same back to him.

In an instant, the fire suddenly flared up, and Timothy reeled back away from it.

"TIMOTHY!" the deer called out to him.

"TIMOTHY, MOTHER NATURE CHARGES YOU WITH CRIMES AGAINST HER!" the deer's boisterous voice said.

Timothy quickly turned to run; his face contorted with fear, and with a silent cry stuck in his throat, but he suddenly found he couldn't move. While he stood there staring at the fire and the deer, the shrubs he had just walked through seemed to have grown in mere seconds into an impenetrable wall. Vines had snuck up between his legs and shackled him at his ankles. The vines tightened, and pulled him back, causing him to stumble and fall back down landing atop a downed tree. He then sat there struggling to free himself from the brambles.

"ENOUGH!" the deer shouted and then began to cough. "Enough, enough, Timothy," he then said, clearing his throat, his voice much softer now as if earlier he was just merely trying to sound bigger and tougher than he truly was.

"What do you want with me?" Timothy asked as he began to sob.

"What do you think I want, Timothy?" the deer said in a much more serious and low tone. "I want to prosecute you. That's my job."

Just then there was a rattling and a rustling in

the bushes, then a moment later a rabbit popped through the wall of shrubs, then a woodchuck, then a gopher.

"Good evening, jurors," the deer said to them. "If you could, just take your seats over there." A mole, snake, and robin soon joined the rabbit, woodchuck, and gopher, and all six of them sat on two adjoining logs just like Timothy had been forced to sit on.

The fire flared up again, and when it died back down Timothy could see a toad sitting on a boulder on the other side of the fire.

"Good evening to you, your honor," the deer beseeched to the bullfrog.

"Yes, yes, good evening to everyone," the bullfrog said mirthfully before letting a croak slip. "Shall we get on with the trial? Let's see what we got here. Okay, here we are, Mother Nature v. Timothy Barren. The charges are thirty-seven counts of murder, eighty-one counts of torture, and one hundred and twenty-six counts of assault. How do you wish to plead, Mr. Barren?"

"WHAT...?" Timothy cried out. **"WHAT ARE YOU TALKING ABOUT?** WHAT THE HELL IS THIS?"

"Please, Mr. Barren, watch your language here in court," the toad said. "Now how do you plead?"

"My client pleads not guilty, your honor," A Weasel said coming through the wall of shrubs. "Sorry, I'm late, sir, but the kids needed to be fed before I left the house."

"Yes, yes, just get on with it," said the bullfrog dismissively.

"Who the heck are you, what is this?" Timothy asked the weasel.

"Haven't you been briefed yet?" responded the weasel in a weaselly voice. "Oh, well, that's a shame, but no bother. Well, let me clue you in, I'm your public defender and you, sir, Mr. Timothy Barren, are about to be charged with crimes against Mother Nature, and what is taking place here is your trial."

"Okay, okay, Mr. Deer make your case," the Honorable Judge Toad requested.

"Why yes, sir, your honor," the deer replied and then walked over to the small woodland creatures that were making up the jury. "Fellow creatures of the forest, I would like to submit to you a plethora of overwhelming evidence along with several testimonies of the victims. That will unequivocally prove to you that not only the defended Timothy Barren is absolute evil, but guilty of crimes against Mother Nature."

"He's good," said the weasel to Timothy. "Never lost a case,"

Timothy sniveled and wiped away frightened tears from his face.

"If it pleases the court, I would like to submit to you exhibit A, a snare young Timothy Barren here had used to capture a poor unsuspecting skunk, and do you know what Timothy did to that skunk after he captured it?"

The jury collectively shook their heads.

"Well, why don't you hear it from Mr. Skunk himself?"

The wall of shrubs shook and rattled before popping out a timid looking skunk. He appeared bruised and bloodied with a gash across the top of his skull, and a broken rear hind leg.

"Awe, this ought to be good," the lawyer weasel said.

The skunk stood next to the toad judge and started to recite his account of what Timothy had done to him. He told the jury about how after Timothy had found him caught up in the snare, he threw rocks at him, probably fearing that if he got too close he would get sprayed. The skunk went on telling all about how Timothy boisterously laughed as he struggled to free himself from the snare. Then, how after the rocks Timothy had thrown at him had left him bloody and bruised, Timothy went into his house to get a container of table salt and threw handfuls of it at him so it would burn in his bloody wounds.

The jury reared back in horror at the skunk's account of what Timothy had done to him.

"Wow, not looking too good for you, Sheesh," the weasel said to Timothy.

"How is this possible?" Timothy sobbed. "He isn't even alive anymore. I buried him in my backyard."

"Oh, well, that's an easy one to answer," stated the weasel. "You see us woodland creatures are pure at heart. Our souls are allowed to come back to testify against jerks like you."

"Your witness, Mr. Weasel," the Honorable Judge Toad said.

The weasel walked up to the skunk and then sniffed the air. "Mr. Skunk can you point-out to the jury who tortured you and ultimately killed you?" asked the weasel.

"Yes," the skunk said. "It was Timothy Barren," and then he pointed a broken arm at Timothy.

A hush fell over the animals of the jury.

"Well, can't argue with that!" cried the weasel. "No more questions your honor."

"WHAT?" Timothy snapped completely shocked and staring wide-eyed at the lawyer weasel as the little mammal sat back down on the log next to him. "You're supposed to be helping me!"

"Yeah, well, I'm not very good at my job," the lawyer weasel admitted. "You know on account that I'm a weasel and all."

Over the course of the next hour the deer brought in several more of Timothy's victims and laid out before the jury quite a few clubs, traps, snares, spears, a magnifying glass Timothy used to burn insects, a brick he had used to smash skulls, a bucket Timothy used to drown poor animals in, a container of poison, and of course Timothy's personal favorite, a can of gasoline. And, with that, the squirrel Timothy had lit on fire just the day before came hobbling up from the dark-depths of the woods. He was still smoking and reeked of singed fur and burnt flesh.

"Mr. Squirrel," said the deer as he looked back at Timothy. "Would you do the court the honor of telling us just what Timothy Barren did to you?"

Timothy felt his heart sink in his chest as he looked over at the squirrel; he then closed his eyes and prayed that this was all a bad dream. "This isn't real... this isn't real... this isn't real," he whispered to himself over and over again as if when he would open his eyes, he would find himself at home snug in his bed.

The lawyer weasel looked at the smoking squirrel and then looked at Timothy. "You did that!?" he said and then shook his head at Timothy. "No, no, no, no, no, not good, not good," he muttered like a teacher tsking his student.

The squirrel opened his mouth to speak, and instead of words, smoke came forth from deep inside him, followed by several heavy coughs.

"Ahhhheeee!" the squirrel wheezed and then brought up a ball of phlegm from deep within his chest. He spit it out and then wiped the spittle that still dangled from his chin with his front paw. "Excuse me," he said. "I haven't been feeling too well as of lately as you can see."

"We understand, Mr. Squirrel," the deer prosecutor said. "Please take your time."

"Yes, well... what did Timothy Barren do to me?" the squirrel began. *"WELL, I'll tell you what Timothy Barren did to me!* Timothy Barren set up a trap right in the path I used every day when I foraged for food. He covered it with leaves and handfuls of grass so I wouldn't see it. And, when I was on my way to collect a few pieces of fresh lettuce for dinner from Timothy's neighbor's garden, I found my let caught up in it."

"What did you do then?" asked the deer.

"What do you think I did? I screamed and tried to free myself. But the more I struggled the more the more exhausted I became. I pulled and pushed on the walls of the cage, but it was of no use. There was no getting out of it. The metal wire walls of the cage eventually dug so deep into my limbs that it had broken my skin, and then when I started to bleed badly, I gave up trying, exhausted."

"What happened then?" asked the deer.

"Then Timothy showed up," the squirrel said, breaking down into a sob. "He started shouting at me 'Got you!' like some kind of psychopath. Then, he grabbed a stick and started poking me, and hitting me atop my head, laughing the whole time.

I struggled and tried the run away from him, *but, the cage held tight around me."*

"I DIDN'T MEAN IT!" Timothy shouted from where he sat on the other side of the fire.

"**IF YOU DIDN'T MEAN IT, THEN WHY DID YOU GO TO GRAB THE CAN OF GAS THEN?**" shouted the squirrel right back at him.

The jurors gasped in horror.

The toad judge called out, "Enough! I will have order in the court of the forest."

Timothy's weasel lawyer looked up at him and told him, "I'm pretty sure you should shut-up now. Badgering the witness won't help your case."

Timothy wiped his nose with the sleeve of his Halloween costume and began to breathe heavily as he worked to choke back his tears.

"Go on, Mr. Squirrel," the toad judge asked.

"Well, after Timothy Barren got done belaboring me with the stick, he said to me, 'I know... I got something for your dumb ass,' and then he disappeared into the shed at the back of the yard, only to reappear with the can of gas."

The squirrel paused not wanting to go on with his testimony.

"Please, Mr. Squirrel," the deer prosecutor said. "Please, finish telling us what Timothy Barren did to you."

The squirrel began to cry, and with a weak voice he said, "He poured the gas on me. It stung my eyes and went into my mouth. I... I... I began to choke on it. I could feel... I could feel it in my nose, burning."

"What happened then, Mr. Squirrel?" asked the deer.

"He lit... He... He... He lit a match, and dropped it on m-m-me," the squirrel burst out into tears, and so did Timothy.

"*And* what happened when the match hit you, Mr. Squirrel?"

"I BURSTED INTO FLAAMMESSS!!!" the squirrel cried out. "I could feel the flames burning me, searing off my fur and flesh. I... I could smell myself cooking. I could feel myself *DYING. And then,* I was gone."

"Ow-www," was the sound the jurors made collectively as they stared at Timothy scornfully.

"No more questions your honor," the deer said, and then he walked back over to his side of the clearing, sat down, and began grooming his genitals with his tongue.

"Your witness, Mr. Weasel," said the toad judge.

"Don't worry kid, I got this," the weasel replied, looking up at Timothy and then giving him a wink. Timothy just put his hands over his face praying this would all go away.

The weasel lawyer stood up and made his way through the clearing, around the fire, and over to the squirrel.

"Mr. Squirrel, can you tell me who did this to you?" the weasel asked.

"Yes, it was Timothy Barren," the squirrel answered him.

"That Timothy Barren?" the weasel then pointed at Timothy.

"Yes."

"Are you sure?"

"Yes."

"And he used that can of gas over there?" the weasel then pointed to the can of gas.

"Yes," the squirrel answered.

"Did it hurt?" asked the weasel.

"Yes, badly," said the squirrel.

"Really?" asked the weasel.

"YES!" said the squirrel.

"*Fuuuccccckkkk,*" said the weasel. "No more questions, your honor."

"You may step down, Mr. Squirrel," the toad judge said with sympathy in his eyes. The squirrel then slunk off back into the woods after the shrubs and bushes had split apart making a path for him.

"*YOU DIDN'T HELP AT ALL!*" shouted Timothy at his lawyer.

"*Well,* I didn't say I was any good," the weasel lawyer responded. "I mean... C'mon, I'm a weasel for Christ's sake."

"I will now ask the members of the jury to go for their deliberation," the toad judge requested.

The jury critters then walked out of the clearing and disappeared into the parting shrubs.

"Wait!" Timothy shouted, standing up from the log. "Don't I get to say something on my behalf?"

"No," said the toad judge as he croaked out laughter. "This is the court of the forest, not the Peoples Court. I'm Judge Hopner, not Judge Whopner," he chuckled.

"Well, see you around kid," Timothy's weasel lawyer said to him before beginning to slink off.

"What?" Timothy cried out, his mouth agape. "Where the hell are you going?"

"Awe, the jury should be coming back in a minute or two, pretty cut and dry case. *Besides,* I don't like sticking around to see myself lose a case. It makes me feel like a loser."

Just then the jury came through the shrubs and re-took their seats in the clearing.

"Have you reached a verdict?" asked the toad judge.

"Yes, your honor," the gopher said working as the head of the jury.

"AND?" asked the toad judge.

"We the jury find Timothy Barren GUILTY on all charges of crimes against Mother Nature."

"NO!" Timothy cried out.

"Tough break, kid," Timothy's weasel lawyer said to him. *"Well, see ya."*

"Well, then with the power invested in me by

the court of the forest, I hear by sentence you, Timothy Barren, to death for crimes against Mother Nature," the toad judge ordered and then he slammed his gable down on the rock he'd been perched upon, the sound echoing throughout the entire forest.

"NO... NO, NO, NO, NO, Noooooo!" Timothy cried. "You can't do this! I'm sorry... I'm sorry... I'll never hurt another animal again. I'll become a vegetarian. I'll volunteer for the ASPCA. I'll do whatever you want. Pleaassseeee... Pleaaasssseeeee... don't do this. I'm sorry. **I'M SOOOORRRRRRRRRYYYYY!!!**"

Timothy sobbed on uncontrollably until he almost passed out, and upon the toad judge seeing him weep, he sighed and said, "Wait... In light of your remorse and you're throwing yourself upon the mercy of the court. I have reconsidered your sentencing."

Timothy looked at the toad judge with his bloodshot eyes.

"I re-sentence you to walk through the tunnel of understanding," said the toad judge banging his gable on the rock again.

"W-what?" Timothy asked totally confused. "What is the tunnel of understanding?"

"It's a tunnel that you're going to have to walk through, and when you do, you're going to find out just what it's like to be one of us, a critter of the forest," the toad judge said. "You're going to understand just how hard it is to be a defenseless creature."

"That's it," Timothy asked beseechingly. "That's it... and then I can go home?"

"Yes, that's it, Timothy," said the toad judge. "Just walk through the tunnel right over there and you can go home."

Timothy looked over to where the toad judge was pointing and he watched the trees and bushes bend and contort making a darkened tunnel that led deeper into the forest.

"O-*okay... Well, goodbye then,*" Timothy said, anxious to leave. He then walked up to the tunnel's entrance and peered past its very edge. He looked around briefly and then looked back at all the woodland creatures that made up the court. He then looked down into the tunnel cautiously thinking that it may be a trap. He felt his stomach tighten and his bowels quake. He didn't want to go into the tunnel, but he knew that the only way to go home was through it, and he sure as hell didn't want to spend any more time where he was.

Timothy stepped into the tunnel, and he could feel the dark all around him. He took a few more steps and then thought about just closing his eyes and running through the tunnel as fast as he could, but then he saw something, it was small and distant, but it was there. *A light...* he thought and then concentrated on it. *Yes... Yes... it was a light, a light at the end of the tunnel.*

Picking up his pace, Timothy hurried himself as fast as he could through the tunnel. He felt himself giddy with joy as the light and the end of the tunnel neared. "I made it! *I'M GONNA MAKE IT!*" he shouted.

When Timothy had reached the end of the tunnel and felt himself engulfed in the light; it was so bright it blinded him. He blinked rapidly trying to regain his sight, and after a moment things began to come back into focus. He could see trees and shrubs, and the blueness of the sky above him. He could feel the warmth of the sunshine on his back, and the coolness of the breeze in the air. He could feel the mud on his arms and legs and feel the water all around him. *I'm in the tarn*, he thought. *Its daylight and I'm still on the edge of the tarn. I must have hit my head when I fell down and been here all night. It was all a bad dream, the court, the toad judge, the squirrel I killed coming back to life to testify against me. It was all just a nightmare brought on by me hitting my head. Oh... Thank God!*

"Coooool," Timothy heard a voice say coming from somewhere behind him. And, before the opportunity had arisen for him to turn around to see from where or from whom the voice was coming from, he felt himself being plucked up off the ground, heading skyward, as if he had been picked up by a giant.

Whaaaat iiissss ttthiiissss, he thought as he felt himself rocket up towards the sky.

"*Hey,* Adam, look what I caught," the voice said.

"What is it?" another voice called out.

"It's a bullfrog!" the voice Timothy knew being Raymond's said enthusiastically.

"Cooooooooolllll... let's stick fire crackers up its ass!" said Adam.

"Oooooh, serves him right, that little jerk hurting them poor defenseless animals the way he did," Ally said.

"Yes, April, that was a good one, I really liked it," Henry added.

"I do have to admit..." Murray began, but then had to pause when the winds picked up causing his candle to almost go out. "Ah... as I was saying... I do have to admit, that story was a lot better than the one you told last year."

"*Oh, wow!*" April exclaimed sarcastically. "I actually got a compliment from the all wonderful storyteller Murray."

"Yah, itt uas a ot bet-tar n thah un oh toold ass ear, Moory," Tilly chided him.

"Oh, shut up, Tilly," Murray snapped. "My story last year about the boy who liked to steal woman's undergarments was a lot better than anything we've heard tonight, so far."

"Oh, no way, nah-ah, you wish, and pffft," were just a few of the collective replies to Murray's assessment of his story.

"I don't care what you morons believe!" Murray pouted derisively. "None of you half-wits could hold a candle up to my storytelling."

"A cinnamon candle?" asked April to the laughs of all the others. Murray didn't dignify her statement with a reply.

"Well, aren't you cute!" they suddenly could hear the old man say to a little girl wearing a bumblebee costume. "You better keep an eye on her or she might fly away, the little angel," he then told the little girl's mother who was holding her hand.

"Sounds like somebody's beers are starting to kick in," Henry quipped.

"Well, at least he's in a *better* mood now," Ally replied bitterly. "I'm sick of him being such a grump all the time."

"What did you expect?" Murray said harshly. "He's like this every year. You would be too if you disliked Halloween and your wife harassed you every year to take part in it."

"He still doesn't have to be such a grouch though," Ally replied back to Murray.

"He's not... just look at him," April said giggling.

There was the old man at the end of the driveway now playing with a wiener dog that'd been dressed up in a costume that made the pup look like a hot dog. The pooch excitedly jumping up on the old man's legs, as its owner than commanded the dog—named Bailey—to get down and behave itself. The old man continued trying to pet the dog as it began to spin around in circles exciting itself into frenzy over the piece of beef jerky the old man was teasing it with.

"Awwwwe, would you look at that," Ally said softly. "He still does have a heart after all."

"Da yawggy emines me ahva peyaches," Tilly mumbled.

"Would you please stop talking, Tilly?" Murray snipped chiding her again. "It's like trying to understand a drunken retard."

"Shut-up, Murray," cried April. "You talk to her that way again, and I'll blow out your candle myself. And, you're right, Tilly, the doggy does look like, Patches."

"Awe, I miss, Patches," Ally said somberly.

"Me too," added Henry.

"Alright, if we're done going down memory lane, shall we get on with it?" asked Murray' "I do believe that I was next, who will be picking for me?"

"Why don't you pick this one, Tilly?" asked April, knowing it would irritate Murray to hear her speak again.

"All-ight," Tilly babbled. "Yets se... Aye cooze ah itch."

"The what?" asked Murray, now trying to play nice after having not wanted any of the other three jack-o-lanterns to give him any grief.

"Ah itch... ofa year, yagging er kid!"

There was a pause and then Ally spoke, "Oh, I see what she's saying. She chooses the witch over there, the one who is dragging her kid around forcefully."

"Yeapp," said Tilly enthusiastically.

All the jack-o'-lanterns turned their attention to the woman across the street that was pulling her child around by the arm, a little girl dressed in a 1950's sock-hop outfit. The little girl was crying that she didn't want to go home already, that they were late starting trick-or-treats because her mother, the woman in the Witch costume, was late coming home from work. The woman then continued jerking the child harshly down the sidewalk, yelling and chiding her as they went, "I don't care if Halloween only comes once every millennium, I said we're going home!"

"Oh, that poor child," said Ally. "It looks like she's got hardly any candy in that bag yet."

"No, mommy!" cried the little girl. We've only gone down one street, we can't go *home* already!

The mother in the witch costume spun herself around grabbing the little girl tightly by her arms and shouting, "You'll do whatever I tell you, *you hear me!*" The little girl then pulled her arms away from her mother, and the woman in the witch costume slapped her across the face before grabbing her hand again forcefully, pulling the little girl along as she wailed out in heartbreak and pain.

"Oh, that woman really is a witch, isn't she?"

April proclaimed.

Just then the old man got up from his chair at the end of the driveway and yelled, "Hey," to the woman in the witch's costume. The woman paid the old man no mind as she kept dragging her daughter along the sidewalk. The old man began to walk across the street and then yelled, "Hey," for a second time. This time the woman dressed up as a witch stopped.

"Yeah, what the *hell* do you want?" she sneered at the old man.

"Just what in Sam hell do you think you're doing?" replied the old man. "Who do you think you are, hitting a defenseless child like that?"

"She's my daughter, now mind your own damn business!" the witch shouted at him.

The old man approached even closer and began pointing a finger at the woman. "You don't do that to your child," he berated the woman. "This is supposed to be her special day. The one day a year that she can go out and have fun. Nobody's supposed to hurt her on this day!" he said as his voice increasingly rose.

"*Well,* I've got a headache and my feet hurt, so I'm going home, and she's coming with me," the witch stated. "And, if you don't like it, *screw you!*" she then stuck her tongue out at the old man.

The little girl in the sock-hop outfit just wiped her eyes with the sleeves of her costume and then stared at the old man.

"*Screw me!*" replied the old man flabbergasted.

"I'll give you a headache you old bag. Don't you ever take this little girl for granted, one day she mightn't be around anymore, and then you'll be sorry. You should cherish every moment you have with her."

"Shut-up, you dumb old twit," the witch woman responded as she continued on down the sidewalk with the little girl in tow.

"Come on now," the old woman said as she came up behind the old man after having gotten up to retrieve him. "Come back to our side of the street and sit back down before you work yourself up into a heart attack."

"Stupid, bitch," the old man mumbled to himself as he turned around facing the old woman who had gently taken his hand. They then headed back to their chairs across the street.

"Well... I guess we know who's had a bit too much of the hard cider tonight," Murray said jokingly.

"Screw you, Murray," Henry snipped at him contentiously. "He had every right to do what he did. I'm just sorry he didn't punch the dumb bitch in the face!"

"You mean witch," Ally implied.

"No, I don't," said Henry.

"Alright, let's just start the story then," April said, trying to mollify the tension between the jack-o'-lanterns. "Murray, I believe it was your turn, and your story is about that witch."

"Yes, yes... Well, the two of them ambled on

down the street after their confrontation with the old man, witch former, child the latter. And, as they made their way back home the witch authoritatively continued to pull on the child's arm as the little girl in the sock-hop costume obstinately refused to concede and go along with her mother's wishes."

"Come along, Jenna... Pick up your feet *or* I swear to *God,* I'll drag you," Jenna's mothers said to her keeping up in her foul morose. Jenna knew that her demur was moot by this point, her mother had made up her mind, *"I said we're going home!"* and there was nothing she could do to change that. But, still, she didn't want her mother's imperious, domineering, narcissistic attitude to go unchallenged, so she kept on with her slow walk, and her small baby steps, knowing that her stoical resolve to her mother's affront would begin to burrow its way under her mother's skin. And, as long as she kept it up, she knew by the time they had made it home, her mother would be so irate and seething on the inside, she would be ready to have an aneurism.

But, Jenna had figured her mother would also be unable to express her frustration or belabor her because all she did was really what her mother told her to do, *go home.* She couldn't help the fact that she was small and her tiny legs couldn't keep up with the determined witch.

When they had made it back to their house, the witch yelled out to a couple of trick-or-treaters who were just then walking up their driveway at the very same time she was, "Go away! We don't have any more candy, Halloween's over now." The children at first thought she was just playing the role of her costume and they carried on to the front door of the home. But then, the witch shouted even more mean-spiritedly at the children, "What did I just say, you little brats! Go on **SCRAM!**" and the children took off running to the next house. Not a single one of them were about to let a real-life witch come between them and their goal of a bounty of sweets which was rightfully theirs, endowed to them by the laws of childhood.

"In the house, NOW!" the witch screamed at Jenna, her voice becoming hoarse with emotion and disgust as it came to a crescendo in a cackle-like croak as she ran out of breath.

Jenna immediately went into the house and ran up to her room at once, slamming the door. The witch then yelled to her from the bottom of the stairs when she'd heard the door slam. "You better watch yourself, Jenna! Don't make me come up there! You won't like me when I'm mad!"

Won't like you when you're mad? Jenna thought. *I don't like you now. Or, when you're drinking, or when you're working and you don't want me to bother you, or when you're on the phone and I make too much noise in the background for your liking, or when you force me to do everything you want to do and never anything I want to do. Hell, I don't even like you when you're happy.*

Jenna turned on her television, and to her surprise there were Halloween specials still playing on one of the networks. She then hopped up onto her bed and poured out the contents of her bag over the coverlets. It was a sorrowful haul indeed. A cache so small she would've been embarrassed to call herself a kid if it were of her own efforts, and not the result of her mother forcing her to come home early.

A few candy bars, a rather small segment of liquorice, three pieces of hard candy, and a gobstopper was all she had to show for a week's worth of digging through the dust-filled, moth-riddled boxes in the attic for the nostalgic clothing she needed to make up her costume.

She felt her stomach begin to growl and thought of the dinner her father had prepared for them before he'd left for work. Spaghetti and meatballs with cheesy garlic bread, her absolute favorite. The very thought of it was now making Jenna's mouth water as she licked her lips in hunger. She silently wished that she would have eaten earlier with her father back when he had just finished cooking it. That was right before he had kissed her on the cheek, told her he loved her, and went off to work the night shift as a paramedic at Saint Christopher's Hospital. But, she was too excited about Halloween to eat then, the anticipation of trick-or-treating being such a short time away filling her every thought with joy. She was a prisoner of imagining all the candy she was going to collect. How her night's haul was going to make Willy Wonka look like a two-bit sugar dealer. So she had elected to forgo dinner with her dad, and now it was too late, it sat forlornly out of reach on the kitchen stovetop in topper ware containers.

Jenna knew that in order to get her hands on the spaghetti and meatballs, she would have to surreptitiously slip back downstairs past the witch and retrieve it without making a sound, and even then it would still be cold. And if, she wanted to have it heated back up, which, of course, would require her mother allowing her to have it in the first place, it would surely entail an apology from her. That meant she would have to swallow her pride and come crawling to the witch, beseechingly asking her if she could do it for her. Because, Jenna still wasn't old-enough to use the stove yet, and the microwave still seemed a little too complicated for her grasp with all of the machine's buttons.

Jenna looked at her candy sullenly. It was in a pile no bigger than what you could fit in the palm of your hand. *Well, at lease it's something to eat,* she thought. Because, going downstairs and asking for some of the spaghetti would have been like Gretel, knowingly walking through the forest only to stumble upon a house made of gingerbread she knew contained a witch, and still knocking on the door anyway. And, besides, Jenna could already hear that her mother was on the phone with somebody important from her work, and any interruption of her conversation by her would be met with a truculent scolding.

After finishing off the candy, and watching an hour of television, Jenna felt her eyelids begin to grow heavy and her consciousness began to waver. What little sugar she had consumed from the candy did nothing to prevent the sandman from creeping in and taking root over her senses.

Meanwhile, downstairs Jenna's mother carried on with her conversation with her boss, Mr. Fergusson, about the missing money that the bookworms down in accounting had just noticed been pilfered from the charity—The Never-Ending Wish Foundation—to which Jenna's mother worked at.

The witch's boss, Mr. Fergusson, didn't accuse as so much as nonchalantly implied, to Jenna's mother that she could possibly be considered a *person of interest* in the disappearance of said funds.

Jenna's mother had been widely known for being a woman whom appreciated possessions of a finer quality, even if such things far exceeded what her income as a treasurer of a non-for-profit charity would allow. Such extravagances, she routinely liked to indulge in would have always remained out of her reach if she hadn't helped herself along at times. Even when her husband's meager income as a paramedic been factored along with hers, it still remained obvious to anybody who knew her that she'd been aided financially in one way or another.

She knew that her lifestyle in which she had flaunted to family, friends, and neighbors didn't leave her in such a strong position to deflect such accusations. And, the fact was, she had stolen from the charity, and everybody knew it. She could see no way to deny that.

The money she took was not only meant to give terminally ill children, one last opportunity to go somewhere fun, perhaps Disney World. But, was also to provide a child with an opportunity to spend a few final days with their family before they became too weak and undoubtedly in agony to leave the hospital and its round the clock care.

But, that is not the only money the witch had taken. She had also dipped into other accounts, those that held funds to help families pay for life-saving operations and Medication. She had taken funds which she was sure probably caused the premature deaths of at least a handful of children over the years.

Finally, having cleaned off all her green makeup, and her costume thrown in the trash, the witch set off into a bottle of wine and a couple of Percocets, courtesy of a high-priced doctor who was all too willing to write prescriptions for his customers who had the means and willingness to pay for his extravagant services. Jenna's mother had been to upset over the phone call she just had with her boss and needed a little something to help take the edge off her shaken nerves. She knew that she shouldn't mix the pills with alcohol, but she had scoffed at it anyways. She desired something strong enough to put her mind at ease and hopefully work as a sedative so she could eventually get some sleep that night.

At just past ten o'clock a thought had occurred to her that it might be in her best interest to call and inform, Richard Brassard, her brother-in-law who was also a criminal defense attorney and tell him all about her problem at work. But it was late, and she didn't want him to know anything unless it was necessary, *and besides,* it was past ten, and he and his wife, Alice, were probably already in bed. They always went to bed early, *such wimps,* she thought.

The witch filled herself up another glass of wine and then thought that it would best to just wait on obtaining a lawyer, at least until the authorities became involved. Besides, it had sounded to her like, her boss, Mr. Fergusson, might be just in the beginning stages of an internal investigation, and was trying to do a little fishing when he'd called.

The witch finished her glass of wine and then climbed up the stairs to check and see if Jenna was still awake. And, if she was, *Lord, help her!* Almost eleven at night and she still hadn't put herself to bed, this wasn't going to stand.

"You mean she doesn't even tuck Jenna into bed at night? That's awful," Ally said, sounding animated.

"Would you please shut up?" Murray sternly snapped at her. "Stop ruining my story, or I'll ruin yours."

"Oh, knock it off, Murray," April said in a huff. "She just got a little carried away with the story, is all. She hasn't hurt anything. You can pick back up right where you left off."

"I beg to differ," Murray complained, taking on a bombastic tone. "She ruined the atmosphere I was building."

"Yeah, well, too bad," Henry snidely quipped at Murray.

"Yeeahh, Oo wad," Tilly repeated.

"What are you boys doing trick-or-treating?" the jack-o'-lanterns heard the old man call out from his seat perched at the end of the driveway. "You boys are too big for this. You should be out chasing girls not candy. Ha!"

"Yeah, well... we like candy," one of the boys snickered back at him.

"Ha! I bet you like a lot of things, just not girls!" proclaimed the old man mockingly.

"*What?* Nuh-uh,*"* replied the boy dumbfounded.

"I think he's calling you a fag, man," said one of the boy's friends who was wearing a Star Trek costume.

"Ha... now there's a quick one," the old man said to the trekker.

"Screw you old man," quipped the boy, and then he and his friend moved on without receiving any candy.

"I knew it!" said the old man. "You're only proving my point, you little daisy."

"Stop that now," said the old woman as she gently slapped the old man on his arm.

"Ahhahaha... those boys did look like a couple of daisies," Murray managed to stammer out as he laughed to himself.

"Oh, leave them alone," April chided him. "You're never too old for trick-or-treating. Besides, I thought you were all in a tizzy to get back to *your* story?"

"Alright, alright," Murray hissed at April. "Now where was I? Oh, yeah,"

The witch cracked open Jenna's bedroom door, peeking in only to find that *indeed* Jenna was sound asleep still in her Halloween costume and surrounded by candy wrappers while the television droned on in a murmur of the late night news.

Having seen the mess and the television left on, the witch threw up her hands dramatically into the air as if to say, *what, can't turn off the TV?* She then crept into the room to power the television down, but had elected to leave Jenna in her costume still lying in and among the candy wrappers. *If that's the way you want to put yourself to bed, Fine,* the witch then thought to herself before she left the room.

After the witch seemed satisfied that Jenna was asleep and would no longer be a burden for the rest of the night, she opened up her second bottle of wine, and popped a few more of her little white pills. She had really thought she needed to up her dose, for the anxiety of potential pending legal troubles kept creeping into her mind and weighing her thoughts down as heavy as stone.

Midnight came calling and the grandfather clock in the living room chimed its twelve dongs. The witch couldn't help but count them off as they went by, *one for every year in prison,* she thought to herself sullenly. *"Why...* Why did I have to do it?" she cried out in a choked voice as she gasped for air. "It wasn't my fault. If they had just paid me what I was worth, none of this would have happened. How did they expect me to live on the pittance they paid me? All that money... all that money *every* day going through my hands, and I wasn't allowed to touch none of it." The witch continued to sob as she finished her glass of wine with two final passionate gulps, and then continued on griping to herself, *as if* in some way, it was consoling.

"The children, the children," she said mockingly. "Everything is always about the children. *WELL, WHAT ABOUT ME?* Don't I matter? They were all as good as dead anyway, and the money wasn't about to do them a damn of good. It was just a waste, really... *It just prolonged their suffering when you really think about It."* she thought justifying her actions. "If anything, I should get a medal for what I did. I helped end all those people's suffering. All the kids, their parents, the doctors and nurses who had to deal with them, and clean up after their sniveling little asses as they wailed, puked, and shit themselves all over the place. These parents should be thanking me for what I did for *them."*

The witch reached for her bottle of wine and then drained the last of it into her glass before dropping *yet* another pill down into the tawny liquid. She then watched as it settled itself at the bottom and began to dissolve. She took another big sip of the bitter liquid and began to say to herself as her speech slurred, "These damn kids with all of *their* problems, who the hell would want them anyways? They come into this world ruining your body, then they suck you dry... not only financially, but spiritually. All that incessant whining—*Mommy, I want this, I want that.* Yeah, *well...* I want you to shut up! Having that kid was the worst mistake I ever made." The witch continued to babble, having become maudlin from the speedball cocktail she'd taken down. It had drowned her brain and had taken over her thoughts. "Why can't she be like one of those *good* brats from the charity, and just drop dead already so I can get my life back?"

The witch stood up from the couch suddenly, and the almost lethal dose of Percocets and alcohol rushed through her bloodstream straight to her brain making her feel dizzy and light-headed. "Whoa, I need to lie down," she stammered, barely even able to get the words out, the drugs pumping through her with every one of her rapid heartbeats.

"It 'ill be alright... It 'ill be alright...," she babbled to herself as sleep slowly took a stranglehold on her. "Screw'em if they can't take a joke," was the last thing she was able to murmur to herself as she slipped from the realm of the conscious to the unconscious.

The witch snored heavily as her body worked overtime to rid itself of the poisons. While she slept, she dreamt of a different life, a life without kids, without worries, without bosses who were willing to call you up at home and ruin your future. She dreamt of a life where money was endless, and she could go on the nicest vacations, and eat at the finest restaurants, and *screw* the best looking men. A life she could have had before she met Robert—Jenna's father—and fell for his good looks, whimsical personality, and all the bullshit he had told her about how he was going to become a surgeon.

The old grandfather clock chimed twice letting any awaken ears know what time it was, and with the gongs the witch became semi-aware of her consciousness. Jenna's mother then repositioned herself on the couch, pulling a blanket that had been neatly placed over the sofa's back down over her head. Soon, a few minutes passed since the clock had chimed and the house began to resettle itself in a veil of all-encompassing silence.

BANG! BANG! A knock on the front door rang throughout the house, but the witch continued to sleep, unperturbed.

BANG! BANG! The knocking struck again, louder this time.

Jenna's mother then tossed and turned on the couch having heard the pounding on the front door, but refusing to acknowledge it, or let it break her out of the paralysis of sleep.

BANG! BANG! BANG! The strikes impinged on the door in rapid succession finally waking the witch up.

"What the heck is this?" the witch groggily asked herself. "Who the *hell* is at the door at this hour? It better not be any more of those damn trick-or-treaters or I will break my foot off in their asses."

The witch staggered to the door, throwing it open without even so much as looking through the peephole first. "Who the *hell* is it? Who the *hell* are you?"

It was a boy, he was as pale as the moon, and he stood before the witch looking completely sullen and emotionless, as if a vampire had drained him of not only his blood but his soul. "I want my heart," the little boy said to her as he looked up at the witch.

"What the hell are you talking about?" the witch bitterly snipped at him and then slammed the door in his face. "Go home, kid. Get the *hell* off my property before I call the cops."

"Fucking kids and their stupid pranks," she muttered to herself before looking up to see the arms of the grandfather clock which stood crookedly before her. "It's past two in the morning already. Where the fuck is these little bastards' parents?"

The witch then went over to the refrigerator to grab some milk as she was feeling dehydrated from all the wine she had drunk.

BANG! BANG! BANG! Those three sudden raps

at the door struck again.

"That little son of a bitch," the witch mumbled as she put the carton of milk down on the counter. "That little shit is dead."

Quickly, the witch raced to the door swinging it open forcefully. "I told you to get the hell out of here!" she shouted but nobody was at the door. The witch looked up perplexed. "What the heck... the little shit must be playing ding-dong ditch now?" she uttered.

Jenna's mother was then about to close the door when she noticed the child in the distance, standing at the end of the yard near the street. He stared at her, ashen in the moonlight.

"I told you to get the *hell* out of here!" the witch shouted at the boy as she stepped out onto the porch. He continued to stare at her. The witch just stared back at him as if he were retarded.

"I want my heart," the little pale boy said to her in a soft voice.

"I don't know what the heck you're talking about, kid, I'm calling the cops," the witch said, and then went back inside the house.

BANG! BANG! BANG! Rang out again as a fist suddenly impinged on the door almost immediately after the witch had closed it, the noise cutting right into Jenna's mother, scaring her to her core.

Determined to lash out at the child and possibly

even strike him, the witch ripped the door back open violently, her hand held high in the air and cocked in an open hand slap position. But before the witch came down with it, she stopped; fore it wasn't the little boy who stood before her any longer, but a little girl. She was every bit as pallid as the little boy had been, and about his age too, it was possible they could have been twins. She looked up at the witch with her voluptuous black eyes, her lips parted by just a small slit, her long black hair curling around her shoulders. The witch said nothing to her, just stared down upon the child, her voice having abandoned her.

"I want to go to Disney World," the little girl said.

"Yeah, me too, kid," replied the witch.

"You stole the money meant to send me to Disney World, and now it's too late for me to go. Why?"

"I don't know what you're talking about, kid," the witch said, shaking her head bombastically at the little girl's implication, but she slowly felt a sense of dread creeping up inside her. "But, it's really late... so why don't you and your little friend stop playing your little games and go home now?"

"I wanna go to Disney World!" the little girl whined. "Why did you steal from me?"

"Just go away!" shouted the witch as she slammed the door.

The witch then went back to the kitchen and grabbed the small plastic bottle which contained the pills that she'd been taking. She read its label as fast as she could, looking for anything that might say that if she took too many, she might experience bad dreams, or hallucinations, or delusions, or *whatever.*

There was nothing.

The witch put down the bottle of pills and then ran her nervous, sketchy hands through her hair pulling on it at its roots. *This is crazy,* she thought. *Just a couple of brats trying to get a rise out of me, that's all.*

"We just want to know why," a little voice said coming from the living room directly in front of her. "Why did you take our money?" said the little voice, and attached to it was a little girl, small, frail, and just as ashen as the children outside had been.

"I couldn't get my dialysis, and my kidneys failed as a result," the little girl said.

"How did you get in my house?" the witch cried out in fear, her voice running away from her. "I'm calling the police," she then said as she opened a kitchen drawer pulling out a large knife.

"Are you going to tell them what you did?" asked the little girl.

"I DIDN'T *DO ANYTHING!*" yelled the witch, and then she raced to the other side of the kitchen in search of the cordless phone that sat in its cradle at the end of the counter. She picked it up and immediately began pressing the buttons for 911 even before she heard a dial tone. The witch put the phone to her ear, and whispered to herself, "Come on... come on, come on, come on...," as she waited for emergency services to pick up on the other end.

"How come I couldn't go to space camp?" a voice on the other end of the line asked.

"What?" uttered the witch pulling the phone away from her ear, she then looked at it as if it were broken.

"I was supposed to go to space camp before I died of leukemia, and you took that from me. You spent the money that'd been meant for me on a fur coat. Why?"

"Because it's *cold* in the winter, and I like to dress in style, *that's why,*" the witch sardonically spoke into the receiver before slamming the phone back down into its cradle.

"You took my liver," another ghostly boy said from behind her, and she spun around wielding the knife before her. "You took my liver, and I died from blood poisoning," he said, pointing an outstretched bluish finger at her.

"Leave me alone!" the witch screamed at the boy. "All of you... leave me alone!" she said as she shakily held the knife out at him.

"I wanna go to Disney World," the little girl who

was outside, but now inside, whined as she stood next to the other little girl in the living room.

"I want my heart," the boy who had first knocked on the door said as a malaise that was hovering next to the little girls filled the room, the child appearing from out of nowhere in its haze.

"I want my trip to the Grand Canyon," a fourth child called out appearing in the living room with the others.

"Give me back my trip to space camp," the little voice over the phone said loudly as if the phone suddenly turned itself on to speakerphone.

"Give me back my medicine," a new voice demanded as another child appeared from the mist to join the others.

"Go AWAY...," the witch screamed hysterically.

"I want my liver," the little boy behind her said. "I want my liver."

"Can I go to Hawaii now?" asked a new girl flashing into existence at the edge of the fog.

"Get away from me.... Get away from *me... ALL OF YOU!*" the witch yelled to the children wielding the knife out before her.

The witch slowly backed away from the kids, careful to keep her knife aimed at them the whole time.

"M-My Keys," she babbled to herself as she searched the outsides of her pockets for them. "Upstairs... They must be upstairs," she whispered to herself as she shifted her gaze to the staircase.

Quickly she moved, but the children stayed where they were. She began climbing the stairs two at a time until she had reached the top. When the witch stepped into her bedroom, she looked around frantically.

"Where are they? Where are they...," she said as she hurried around the room checking the nightstand and the top of her dresser where she would commonly leave them, but to no avail, they were missing.

"Come on, COME ON...," the witch cried as she began throwing the blankets from her bed thinking that they may have fallen from her pocket when she had lain down after coming home from work earlier that day.

"Are you looking for these?" an eerie little voice said from behind her.

The witch spun around to see the ghost of a girl standing behind her. She was just as white and transparent as the others and her eyes just as void of life and as black as oil. She stood before the witch with an outstretched arm and at the end of her finger tip hung the witch's car keys.

"Give me those!" the witch commanded while jabbing her knife in the air towards her.

"I don't want what doesn't belong to *me*," the ghostly little girl told the witch. Her translucent body fading in and out of the fog that began filling in around her feet.

The witch stepped forward, one arm cocked back ready to lunge forward with a piercing stab, the other reaching out for the keys.

"You just stay right there now," the witch ordered the girl, "No sudden movements, alright?" The girl did as she was told.

The witch grabbed the keys from the girl's hand, then began making her way inch-by-inch around the child heading towards the door.

"Can I have my medicine now?" the girl asked, "I can't breathe without my medicine."

"I don't have your medicine," the witch told her sounding disdainful. "I never had *your* medicine."

"But you stole the money that was meant for my medicine. Money for medicine my mama couldn't afford because she's only a maid. I gave you what you wanted back... Why can't I have what you took from me back?"

"You're dead, kid," the witch said, shaking her head sympathetically at the girl. "You're dead, can't you see that... The medicines not going to do you any good anymore, so just go away."

The little girl just stared at the witch but remained emotionless, silent. Quickly, the witch turned away from her to begin heading for the stairs and ultimately the front door. At the edge of the top of the stairs, though, she stopped before making her way down, peering over towards

Jenna's room. She had forgotten all about Jenna, who she figured by now was either still sound asleep in her bed or dead, murdered by these spirits. The witch fleetingly thought about going into the room and grabbing her daughter from her slumber, wrapping her up in one of the coverlets and running out the front door together. The witch then shook her head mumbling, *the hell with her.*

When the witch turned to head down the stairs the children were there, dozens of them encompassing the entire flight of the staircase, their mouths agape exposing their sharp, pointed, razor-like teeth.

The witch lost her balance upon seeing them, slipping off the first run of the staircase when she saw the children standing there so very close and reaching for her with their claws. She didn't even have time to scream before she was already on her way down passing through the mist that made up the children's presence, dispersing it like it was nothing more than smoke being exhaled. She put out her arms to break her fall and protect her face. But, as she tumbled the knife she'd been carrying in her right hand shifted and pointed back on her when her hand struck the staircase and her wrist bent back. The knife began embedding itself having caught her chin's underside when the witch had slammed down hard upon the staircase.

She slid down to the next step, and the knife

drove itself deeper into her chin. She then hit the step after that and the knife pierced through her jaw and into her tongue. The next step pushed it even further up into the roof of her mouth.

The children disappeared into vapor as she continued to tumble and by the third to last step of the staircase the knife was firmly working its way up through the witch's jaw inching its way closer to its hilt, soon severing her tongue, and making its way into her sinuses. With the pressure put on the knife from being slammed into the second to last step, the knife began cutting into her brain. With the last step it entered her brain fully. Then, when the witch had finally hit the floor, the knife buried itself completely in her skull like it had entered into its sheath. By then it had severed her brain in two, only stopping because its hilt had reached her jaw bone.

The witch lay dead at the bottom of the stairs, her blood flowing freely from out her throats bottom like somebody had left a tap turned on. Her crimson liquid beginning to pool on the white tile floors like spilled paint.

From up at the top of the stairs, the sounds of a bedroom door could be heard slowly creaking open. Behind the door stood Jenna, sleepy faced and peering out down the hall after having been awakened when her mother plunged down the stairs. Jenna then tipped-toed out of her room making her way to the edge of the staircase where she then rubbed the cobwebs from her eyes and waited for her vision to adjust to the light before heading down.

Half way down the steps she noticed her mother's body at the base of the stairs and she stared at it. Jenna then took a deep breath before continuing to head down being careful not to step on her mother's corpse as she slipped past. When she hit the floor she made a quick little leap over the crimson pool of blood, its irony smell reminding her of liver and onions a favorite of her father's which the very thought of food began making her hungry.

The spaghetti and meatballs still sat atop the stove, and Jenna grabbed herself a plate and filled it high before popping it into the microwave, hitting several buttons and managing to turn it on. She then sat at the kitchen table eating her very late dinner and enjoyed every bite of it before heading back to bed.

"Damn... as much as I hate to admit it... that was a pretty good story, Murray," said April approvingly.

"Yeah, that was pretty good. Maybe even the best one so far," Henry agreed. "But you're still a jerk, Murray."

"YE-ah, yair sill a yerk, Merreee," repeated

Tilly.

"Ugh... what did I tell you about talking, Tilly?" Murray said with an air of superiority. "Thank *God* we don't have to listen to any story come out of you tonight."

"Oh, stuff it, Murray," Ally said in a raised voice chiding him once again. "Don't get all high and mighty because you told a good story. It's not like it was the best one here tonight."

"Yes, it was," replied Murray.

"No... it wasn't," quipped Ally. "I still have to go."

"Oh, this ought to be good." Murray grumbled. "What better way to cap off the evening then with a story about ponies and rainbows and magic wishes coming true. Yeah, that's really going to top my story and put an exclamation point on this night."

Just then the pumpkins heard the old man down at the end of the drive asking the old woman to grab him another beer. She had been on her way up to the house to get more candy for the remaining trick-or-treaters that may arise.

"You've had enough beer already," the old woman said, calling back to the old man. "Besides, it's getting late and Halloween will be over soon anyway. The kids on the street are already starting to dwindle."

"All the reason to have one more beer!" whined the old man.

"No!" shouted the old woman from the porch as she stood next to the pumpkins who were trying desperately not to give themselves up by laughing.

"Ah... you're no fun," said the old man throwing a hand up in the air in a show of frustration. "You *say* you're fun... But you are *no* fun."

"Well, now that he's cut off, he should settle down and be just about done for the evening," Henry said in a low voice once the old woman ducked into the house.

"Yeah, it looks like he's already settling down to pass-out," April added and the rest of the pumpkins glanced towards the end of the drive to see the old man already giving into head nods. His noggin rolling back and forth and around on his shoulders like it was on a swivel.

"Maybe we should finish up too then?" said Henry. "Ally, I believe it was your turn."

"Yep, Aweez urn," Tilly confirmed.

"Tilly!" shouted Murray derisively.

"Shhutt Up! Meriey," Tilly responded. "Yo ah-ed, Ahwee."

"Thank you, Tilly, I'll do just that...," said Ally. "Now who is it that needs to pick my character?"

"I haven't picked one yet, I'll go," April stated.

Just then the old woman came back out on the porch with the remaining candy she had left for the trick-or-treaters. The pumpkins remained silent as the old woman eased her tired and arthritic body down the steps of the front porch before making her way over to the old man who was already busy snoring away in his chair.

"Okay... it looks like we might have time for one

more so make it a good one, Ally," April said still using a low tone as if the old woman was still right next to them on the porch. "Your character will be... will be..." April paused for a long moment, and just before Murray was going to say something to her she started in again, "Oh, my god... it's him."

"It is who?" asked Henry.

"Him!" said April. "Over there... across the street—wearing the clown suit."

"Oh, my, I think it *is* him," said Henry.

"Yeh, ieh isz," Tilly agreed. And, this time Murray didn't say a word to her about speaking.

"I'd know that wicked smile of his anywhere, we should do something," Henry demanded.

"Like what?" Murray asked earnestly. "What could we possibly do now? Besides, that was years ago. None of us are even sure of what he may look like anymore. We probably have the wrong guy. You should just go on with your story, Ally. Let's just get this night over with."

The pumpkins grumbled amongst each other, but ultimately they knew Murray was right. Finally Ally agreed, saying, "Fine. I will go on with my story."

"His name is Alan Monroe but some kids now him as a clown, others a magician. We knew him as a cowboy."

Alan Monroe always had a thing for Halloween. Maybe, it was the candy or the dressing up, but Alan didn't think so. Alan had always known what it was. It was death. It was the one day a year where it's been said that the dead could come back to roam the Earth. Also, it happened to be the one day a year were Alan could get away with thinking and even acting out his disgustingly depraved thoughts without feeling guilty about them. To Alan, Halloween was nothing more than a free pass. A pass he would get once a year that would allow him immunity to let his true self come forward and torment the world.

Alan had always been a runt as a child because of his weakened immune system. He was a foot short for his age and where other children were able to go outside and play on colder days, Alan had to stay indoors for fear coming down with pneumonia. It was an ailment he had a knack for contracting which had landed him in the hospital several times before.

As Alan sat forlorn at his bedroom window watching the other children play hide-and-go-seek or two-hand touch football in the street, he had to settle for being a distant spectator.

And, when the neighborhood children would eventually catch on to Alan watching them from his perch high in his second-story bedroom window, they would give him the finger or stick out their tongues at him and shout obscenities his way.

Things weren't much better for Alan even when he'd be allowed to go outside. He would offend have to sneak around the neighborhood and not be seen for fear being bullied and ostracized.

Not being accepted by the other children only made Alan turn inward to escape. Escape from his body. Escape from his bedroom. Escape from his boredom. Alan's fantasies became an outlet for him. They became a way for him to imagine himself as someone else, somebody powerful, strong, and courageous. It also allowed him to be somebody cruel, mean, and vengeful.

Alan committed his first murder when he was only twenty years old. He had drowned a ten-year-old boy named Colin Matthews in the creek not far from his house after he'd smacked Colin on the head with a brick. It happened to be winter time and when the police found Colin's body under the ice... they determined wrongly that it was an accident. That Colin had slipped on the ice and hit his head on the ground before slipping into the water.

The close call with getting caught scared and thrilled Alan at the same time, and from that moment forward he knew he had to be more careful.

Over the years since that first murder, Alan had continued in his sickening downward spiral into insanity. He had convinced himself that by killing his victims on Halloween—Devils' Night—he was somehow not responsible for his actions. That, the killings, he would partake in would somehow be out of his control because it was Halloween and therefore not his fault.

Alan Monroe had even picked up the clown costume that he had decided he would go as this Halloween from a local party store. He had figured dressing up like a happy clown would be a good lure that would attract children to him, plus the make-up would work well at disguising his face.

His plan was simple, just to mingle in with the local kids as they made their way down the streets trick-or-treating. Then, when he had the children's attention during the magic tricks he would perform for them, he would quickly slip a piece of his poison laced candy into their bags. He made sure that it was always something good, something children always wanted to eat first so he could maximize his kills.

It wasn't the first time Alan Monroe had poisoned children... In fact, he had tried it for the first time more than twenty-five years ago when he had poisoned the Duval kids. News of the five Duval children suddenly dying ripped through the heart of the town like a tornado.

"Ohhh... I don't like this part of the story," April said cutting into Ally's story.

"Knee neider," said Tilly.

"Would you two shut-up," harped Murray. "Go

on, Ally, let me know when it gets good."
"Bite me, Murray," Ally quipped.

Alan had dressed up like a cowboy that night when he poisoned the Duval children—his costume complete with chaps and duel colt 45 cap guns on his hips. He walked up and down the darkened streets of his little town looking for his victims—children unaccompanied by parents.

When he had come across the Duval kids, he had no problem what-so-ever gaining their attention, especially the smallest and youngest of them. A series of rope tricks Alan did with his lasso kept the brown-haired, brown-eyed little girl glued to him like she was in a trance. It was only when her oldest brother—a cranky little shit—insisted that they be on their way, did Alan tip his hat and then whistle his way into the night's darkness. But, it weren't before he had handed each of the kids a candy bar laced with arsenic from his leather satchel.

After hearing about how the Duval children becoming violently ill and having suffered horrifically before succumbing to the poison—Alan could hardly contain his giddiness. He then poisoned children again in the same manner the very next year, this time in another state, though. He made sure he was careful not to stay in the same place for too long, that way he could throw off the authorities. And, his absence helped to convince the people of the naive little town that he had victimized, that the killer had moved on.

Over the years Alan had come up with different ways of luring his victims. He was once dressed as a soldier... another year a baseball player, even Big Bird once. But that plan had backfired on him when the only children he could attract were one's young enough to still be accompanied by their parents.

Alan had also experimented with different methods of slaughtering his victims. He had sliced-and-diced a kid one year when he had dressed up as a butcher. Another year he had beaten a child to a bloody pulp when he had dressed up as a boxer. He had even buried a child alive once when he had dressed up as a convict whose job it was to dig ditches in a chain gang as punishment for his crimes. But, none of those murders had given him the thrill that he'd felt twenty-five years ago when he had poisoned the Duval children.

So here Alan found himself, back in his hometown again, this time dressed like a clown, with a pocket full of poisoned candy, looking for another unsuspecting child to murder. Only this time wouldn't turn out like Alan had hoped.

On all Hallows eve it *was* possible for the dead to make contact with the living. And, what Alan didn't know... was that right at that very moment while he was ambling up and down the neighborhood streets in his over-sized clown shoes, looking for his night's fun, several blocks away a stirring was happening to the ground in the local cemetery. A stirring just below the graves marked Duval.

Breaking up through the cool autumn ground were tiny hands that began reaching for the night's sky. As they worked feverishly to dig themselves free of their eternal slumber a miasma wafted from their tattered clothes and mummified flesh. Slowly a sound started to emanate from their throats that hadn't been heard in twenty-five years. It was the sound of anguish and torment, the sound of despair and revenge.

They shambled their way through the cemetery illuminated only by moonlight. Their bones cracked and creaked as they made their way to the street. They then headed up the dusty county road in search of the tiny community that lay just beyond the hills.

Alan, becoming irritated at not being able to find his perfect victim, and as a result had made his way through the neighborhood dejectedly. He was almost all set to give up—but then. But then there she was... A perfect angel in her angel costume and accompanied only by what appeared to be her big sister who was not terribly much older than she was.

A smile came to the clown's face that stretched

comically almost ear to ear. "Yes... Yes, she will do just fine," Alan whispered, and then began to make his way over to her since she was still several houses away from him.

He waited for his angel to approach where the street took a wide turn and there was a gap between houses filled in by a copse of apple trees. The light was dim there, the nearest street lamp having been another thirty yards behind him.

Alan waited patiently as his angel neared and then stepped out from the shadows just when the girls were about to pass.

"Oh, my God!" the older girl gasped when she'd seen the clown.

"Look, Carrie, it's a clown," the little angel said beaming at the sight of Alan.

"Yes, it's a clown," said the big sister. "Now let's go."

"No, wait...," said Alan as he did his best goofy sounding clown voice. "Happy Halloween to you girls, would you like to see some tricks?"

"Oh, please, Carrie, please can we see some tricks?" the angel pleaded. "It will only be a couple of minutes."

"Yeah, please, Carrie...," Alan chimed in helping the angel to double team her big sister.

"Oh, alright, but only for a few minutes," Carrie sighed. "Mom and Dad are expecting us home soon."

"Yea!" was the collective cry coming out of both the little angel and Alan at the same time.

It was on, and Alan knew he only had mere moments, a few minutes at best to work his magic. He started off by pulling a bouquet of fake flowers from his tightly wadded fist, to which the angel clapped her hands at the sight of them appearing out of thin air. He then offered the flowers to the big sister, but when she went to take them from him, at the core of the bouquet a stream of water flew from the flowers hitting her in the face. The little angel erupted into laughter. "Ha-Ha, very funny," the big sister said, wiping her face dry with her jacket's sleeve.

Next, Alan asked the little angel what her favorite animal was. She excitedly told him that it was a giraffe. Alan then pulled out a long, limp, red balloon and with a deep breath blew it into a tube. He then wrangled it in his hands, twisting and pulling it every which way until it almost burst. Finally, with a, "Wah-la," he presented the little angel with her giraffe, which didn't look much like a giraffe at all, but she didn't care, she was too excited to even notice.

"Look, Carrie, a giraffe," the little angel said, holding it up so her sister could see.

Carrie took one look at the mangled balloon giraffe—which reminded her more of the picture of an Ebola virus she'd seen in a National Geographic than a giraffe—and said, "That's great, but we really do have to get going now, so good-bye."

As Carrie grabbed the little angel by the hand and began guiding her towards home, Alan beginning to panic at the thought of the little angel getting away called out to the girls in a hurried voice, "Wait... wait, I almost forgot."

The girls turned around abruptly to see the clown reaching into his knapsack that he had slung over his shoulder. After a moment Alan fished out the poisoned candy bars and offered one to each of the girls. "Here ya go, young ladies, Happy Halloween."

Carrie hesitated to take the candy at first and thought about telling the clown "No thanks," but before she could even say anything the little angel had leaned forward to take the chocolate bar from the clown. But just as the tips of the little angel's fingers felt the smooth edge of the candy bars wrapper, the night's calm and silence they had been experiencing in that dark little section of roadway was suddenly halted. A hand had come lunging out of the darkness grabbing Alan by his wrist and pulling the candy bar back from the little angel's grasp.

Carrie, the little angel, and Alan all stared at the stranger's cold rotted hand simultaneously—then peering up to see whom the hand belonged to.

The stranger's face was gaunt, sunken and

hallow from twenty-five years of being in the ground. Parts of his skull showed through his scalp where his brown hair had once been, and his eye sockets seemed empty and dark like a void. He wore a tattered and torn up suit that barely still clung to his exposed bones and petrified flesh. He was young... or had been young once, possibly not much older than Carrie.

The little angel screamed at the sight of the dead boy and then flung herself face-first into her older sister's arms.

Carrie started to inch away from the clown and corpse, but ended up backing up right into another one. This time it was a girl... maybe all of eight-years-old at the time of her death. She was still wearing the white gown she'd been buried in and appeared extremely decomposed, just as bad as the male.

Carrie quickly pulled herself and the little angel back away from the dead little girl and stared at her—her face frozen in terror.

"Poison...," the corpse of the dead boy wheezed weakly as he squeezed down on Alan's hand like a vise.

Alan cried out softly when the dead boy crushed down on his bones, his voice leaving him and being replaced by muted terror.

"Poison," said the dead girl repeating what the dead boy had just said as she inched closer to the clown.

"Poison...," another boy zombie called out from the shadows, and then stepping forward into the wash of the street lamps. He was soon followed by a fourth and then a fifth trailing close behind, both of them young girls.

"What do you want?" Alan cried out finding his voice again.

"Poison," the larger of the dead boys rasped as he struggled to push stale air out through his rotted voice box. He then pulled Alan's hand up to his face, causing Alan to drop the laced candy bars.

"Poison," cried out the smallest of the dead little girls and then she tripped over her dingy dirt covered gown that she wore.

"Poison," the brown-haired dead boy then grumbled again before sinking his gnarled and blackened teeth around Alan's fingers, severing two of them off at the base of his hand.

Alan screamed out in agony, and the little angel buried herself further into her big sisters chest at the sound he had made.

The tallest of the dead girls was next to sink purchase on Alan's flesh, biting him on his bicep as the brown-haired boy zombie continued to remove fingers.

The other boy's corpse shuffled forward, grabbing hold of the clown's other arm in his waxy, scaly hands. "Poison...," he said, choking out his words right before he slammed his equally blackened teeth down into the supple flesh of Alan's shoulder.

Alan, wincing from the pain, and quickly began to feel himself fall into shock. His legs then began to buckle and shake as the two smallest of the dead girls began to go to work on them.

Carrie watched as the littlest of the female zombies with incredible strength ripped the clown's left foot from his body like a Doberman tearing into a drumstick from a turkey.

The five dead children continued tearing into Alan's limbs feverishly. Carrie watching in horror could only hear the sounds of the zombies choking down the clown's flesh, which muted what was left of their expired voices. The only sound Alan could hear was the sound of his own voice fading as he slipped into unconsciousness.

From the darkness came a light and Alan began to blink rapidly at its sharpness.

"Oh, you're awake," he then heard a voice say from somewhere in the distance.

Alan tried to reach up to rub his aching eyes, but couldn't feel either of his arms move. As his vision focused more clearly he could see that he was in a hospital bed—his arms gone from the shoulders down.

"Wh-What...," he tried to utter, but before he could get the words out another voice said, "Try not to talk. You've been through a serious trauma."

"What... What happened?" Alan pleadingly asked the man who appeared to be a doctor.

"We don't know," he said and then sighed. "You were found unconscious and bleeding in the middle of a roadway more than a week ago. Something gnawed off your limbs. We suspect it may have been coyotes or another pack of wild animals."

"But... But, how? Why?" Alan muttered before becoming weak and needing to close his eyes.

"Try to relax," said the doctor. "There's also something else we need to talk about." The doctor then paused and pulled up a stool next to Alan's bed—sitting down. "Alan," said the doctor tentatively. "You were found with a satchel of candy laced with arsenic that we believe may possibly have been used in the murders of five children right here in this town twenty-five years ago. A police search of your house also came up with evidence of many other child murders that have gone unsolved over the last quarter century."

"So, I've got no arms, no legs, and I'm going to jail!" Alan cried out as he began to sob, his eyes flooding with tears.

"Well... Yes, you would be if...," the doctor began but then cut himself off.

"If what?" asked Alan.

"Well, the thing is... the thing is that we found

something in your blood, some type of poison," the doctor said, sounding a little dumbfounded.

"What kind of poison?" Alan asked.

"We don't know, but we do know what it is doing," the doctor told him and then paused again before standing up. He then grabbed a hold of the blanket that had covered Alan's torso all the way to his neck and yanked it down exposing Alan's naked body.

"The poison is causing you to rot from the inside out," said the doctor.

"Wha-what?" replied Alan terror-stricken as he gazed over what was left of his body which was now turning black in different areas. "You mean I'm just going to rot until I'm dead?" he asked, barely able to stammer out his words.

"No, that's the thing, Alan," the doctor said with an air of smugness to his voice. "You already are dead, Alan. Welcome to Hell."

And, with that, the doctor left the room and then all the corpses of *every* child Alan had ever killed started shambling inside surrounding him on his bed. They bit down, feasting on his flesh for all of eternity, and all Alan ever knew from that point forward was pain, fear, and regret.

"Yeaaa, we finally got that bastard!" cried April.

"Wow! I really think you take the top spot this year, Ally," said Henry.

"She doesn't take it," whined Murray. "Mine was better."

"Uh-uh," said Tilly.

"In your dreams," added April.

"Yes, it was," argued Murray. "Mine was better."

"Okay... I know how to settle this," said Henry. "All those in favor of Murray's story say Yea."

Silence.

"All those in favor of Ally's story,"

A unanimous cry of Yea went up.

"There it's settled," proclaimed Henry. "Ally's the winner this year!"

"But that's unfair. You're all bias because I kept making fun of Tilly. You all agreed just to spite—"

"Shh!" hushed April. "They're coming."

A very groggy old man shuffled past the jack-o'-lanterns on his way into the house and then off to bed. He was soon followed up the porch by the old woman who helped guide him up the staircase to the second floor of their home.

"Next year I'm not going to let any one of you have a turn at telling a story if you're all going to cheat," whined Murray once he knew it was safe to talk again.

"Yeah, you say the same thing every year, so...," responded Ally.

"Shhh," whispered April. "She's coming again."

The old women entered back out on the porch where she approached the jack-o'-lanterns. She then carefully pulled the top from the largest one, bent down, and gently blew out its candle. Its scent of cinnamon mixed with smoke immediately filling the air soon after its flame had extinguished. She repeated the process with the next three leaving the little jack-o'-lantern with the upside down face for last. As the old woman bent down blowing out its candle, thoughts of her youngest daughter and how much she used to love Halloween entered her mind. With a sigh and a good breath, she extinguished the flame before heading inside, only pausing briefly when she thought she heard a small voice say, "Good-night, Mom."

Word-of-mouth is crucial for any author to succeed. If you enjoyed the book, please leave a review on Amazon. Even if it's just a sentence or two, it would make all the difference and would be very much appreciated. You can leave a review by clicking on this link:

http://www.amazon.com/Forest-Light-Dark-Mark-Kasniak-ebook/dp/B01603WX7I/ref=sr_1_1?ie=UTF8&qid=1449807750&sr=8-1&keywords=mark+kasniak

Author's Note

First and foremost, I would like to thank you for purchasing this book! And, if you've gotten it for free, well... Score for you and still thanks for reading it. There is no purpose what-so-ever of having created a story if there is nobody to enjoy it.

As an independent author, I, like many of us out there, are subject to tackling every segment of the production process involved in the making of our novels. Unfortunately though, for a lot of us, we just do not have the resources available to hire professional editors, beta readers, cover designers etc. With that in mind mistakes can and will sometimes happen. Nobody is perfect. So, I am respectfully requesting, that you, the reader, would do me the goodwill of acknowledging to me any errors found in my text, whether it be in the storyline or grammatically, before leaving any negative review. I can be reached at mkasniak@yahoo.com.

I do however fully understand that reviews are part of the writing and marketing process for any author, and in being so I would like to strongly urge you to leave a review of this book on Amazon or anywhere else of your choosing. You can reach my Amazon review page here.

http://www.amazon.com/Autumn-Havest-celebration-Halloween-Macbre-ebook/dp/B018KRSUCY/ref=sr_1_2?ie=UTF8&qid=14502 07277&sr=8-2&keywords=mark+kasniak

I would also appreciate you leaving an honest review of any of my other books based on your enjoyment of them whether good or bad.
Again, thank you.

Please sign up for my mailing list to receive free giveaways, promotions, and information on my upcoming releases. You can sign up here.

http://eepurl.com/bKt0Wr

Other books by Mark Kasniak

In the Forest of Light and Dark

Autumn Harvest… A Celebration of Halloween and the Macabre

Lovienthal Montague Spiritual Detective
A Zombie Novel

Coming soon…

Michael
A continuum of In the Forest of Light and Dark

The Hunger

The Volunteers

Kayla's Story

Ashland

The good, the bad, and the Lovienthal

Acknowledgments

I would like to take this opportunity to thank Chiaralily from the Flickr community in the use of the cover art you see on this book's cover. You can follow her at https://www.flickr.com/photos/chiaralily/

I would also like to thank Shane McClane for being a Beta in the creation of this book.

Manufactured by Amazon.ca
Acheson, AB